In one eye-blinking instant, he was out of the chair and in front of her and grasping her sweatshirt with one fist while the other fist yanked on her hair. She cried out in pain, but he was dragging her over to the box. Yanking the door open. Pushing her inside, face first.

The door slammed, taking the little bit of light with it.

She was inside the tall narrow coffin.

And she was locked in.

Terrifying thrillers by Diane Hoh:

NIGHTMARE HALL

The Coffin

DIANE HOH

SCHOLASTIC INC.
New York Toronto London Auckland Sydney

No part of this publication may be reproduced in whole or in part, or stored in a retrieval system, or transmitted in any form or by any means, electronic, mechanical, photocopying, recording, or otherwise, without written permission of the publisher. For information regarding permission, write to Scholastic Inc., 555 Broadway, New York, NY 10012.

ISBN 0-590-20297-9

12 11 10 9 8 7 6 5 4 3 2 1   5 6 7 8 9/9 0/0

Printed in the U.S.A.   01

First Scholastic printing, January 1995

The Coffin

Prologue

Air.

I need air.

Every time they put me in this dark, narrow, airless space, they insist, as I struggle and scream in fury at them, that there is plenty of air.

But they lie.

It is always the same. In only minutes, my chest begins to ache, as if giant claws are squeezing it. My head hurts as my lungs struggle to pull in enough oxygen. I feel dizzy, as if I've been spinning in circles for hours.

But I haven't been. Because there isn't enough room in my dark, musty chamber to spin, or even to walk. Not enough room to take two steps forward or two steps backward. No room to lie down, and sitting is almost impossible in this tall, dark, narrow, box, unless you scrunch up your legs so that your knees are jabbing into your stomach like cattle prods. A very painful position, and those times when I've been forgotten in here and had been sitting like that, I was totally unable to walk when they finally remembered and came to let me out. My legs had frozen in their folded-up position. They had to reach in and lift me out. I'm not exactly lightweight, and they had a hard time. That made them mad. But it was their fault for forgetting me.

Dark. It is so completely black, as if I'd suddenly gone blind. There are no windows in my box, not so much as a tiny crack to let in a sliver of light from the hall outside. And it is quiet, deathly quiet. The wood is thick. Only the loudest sounds penetrate, sounding vague and distant, as if my ears were stuffed with cotton. Faint voices, an unrecognizable note or two of music, occasional muffled footsteps. This place is almost soundproof.

Which makes it as lonely as an isolated mountaintop in Tibet, or the very depths of an ocean, unoccupied by even the bravest of sea creatures.

The sense of isolation is unbearable.

But that's their goal, isn't it? To make it unbearable.

They've succeeded.

It stinks in here, too. The smell of human panic is everywhere, oozing from the gray-brown boards. Some of the smell is probably mine, past and present.

Once . . . maybe it was the first time they locked me in here . . . I broke every fingernail, ripped them to shreds, trying to claw my way out. And once . . . maybe that was the first time, I had no voice left when they finally set me free. Couldn't talk above a whisper for three days, from the shouting and screaming to be let out.

Air. I need air.

I won't forget this. It won't be forgiven. Ever. It should never have happened to me. I didn't deserve it. It wasn't necessary.

That's what I get for trusting.

Never again. I've learned my lesson, here in my dark, silent, torture chamber. Trust is for fools. I will never be that foolish again. Never.

I won't always be trapped in this small, airless hellhole. I'll be free soon. Free to go about my business.

The business of getting even. Payback time.

I know exactly how to go about it. I have a

plan. A wonderful plan. Thinking about carrying it out has kept me from going insane in this loathsome place.

But first, I have to get out. I have to be freed from this medieval nightmare. This obscene box.

This coffin.

Chapter 1

The woman standing at the sink in the bright, sunny, blue and white kitchen was short but sturdy, with a broad, solid back and plump shoulders. Wiry, graying hair fought to escape the confines of a brightly printed yellow and rust bandana that matched both the woman's cotton dress and her full-length apron. She had made the outfit herself and was very fond of it, even though her best friend, Sunshine Mooney, had said, "My heavens, Mave, in that get-up, you look like a bunch of bananas going bad!" Silver hoops dangled from Mavis's ears and matching silver bangles dotted her thick wrists as age-spotted hands scrubbed at a teabag stain in the bottom of the white porcelain sink.

A country song whined from the black portable radio sitting on the blue-tiled counter at Mavis's elbow. As she scrubbed, she sang along with it, at the top of her lungs, in a nasal, off-key voice.

A pair of hummingbirds hovered at the feeder outside the wide window above the sink. Every few minutes Mavis, continuing to scrub diligently, would glance up from her task and gaze in wonder at the tiny, busy birds. "Most amazing thing I've ever seen," she would murmur in awe, "no bigger than some insects I've seen in my time. But so much prettier. Amazing!" Then she would resume her discordant vocalizing.

People who had heard Mavis sing said, "Well, Mavis couldn't carry a tune in a wheelbarrow, but she sure is loud." This was true, as Mavis herself laughingly admitted.

But on this particular, beautiful, early-spring morning, the volume at which Mavis sang her favorite country tune would be her undoing. Because her heartfelt caterwauling kept her from hearing the black metal latch on the back door lift upward surreptitiously, making the telltale clanking sound that it always made.

If Mavis hadn't been shaking the thick, wooden, kitchen ceiling beams with her voice, she might have heard that telltale clanking sound.

And she might have been saved.

But because she was wailing, "You-oo hurt me so-oo bad!" at the top of her lungs, Mavis failed to hear that telltale clank, or the ensuing creak of the metal hinge as the back door swung open, or the soft, whispery footsteps entering from the small, enclosed back porch that housed a freezer, an old wicker chair and table, and a collection of house plants. Her back to the kitchen, she never heard the footsteps crossing the blue and white squares of floor tile and tiptoeing up behind her.

Lost in the song, Mavis failed to sense a new presence in the room. She was unaware of any approaching danger until it was too late. Cruel and powerful hands encircled her throat from behind, cutting into her windpipe and abruptly ending her song in mid-note.

The hummingbirds outside the kitchen window went on about their business, unperturbed as Mavis, with strength surprising for her age, struggled valiantly for her life.

In spite of her surprising strength, she struggled in vain.

When the last breath of air had been cruelly choked from her body, she gave one last, despairing sigh and went completely limp, like the wet dishrag still clutched in her left hand.

A voice behind her whispered, "Done! Took long enough. Tough old crow! Now, what am

I going to do with you? Can't have the lady of the house tripping over you when she comes home."

Eyes cold with a lack of emotion glanced around the sunny room. The inert corpse in garish rust and yellow sagged to the floor. "Ah, yes," the whisper said triumphantly, "I see the perfect place. Come along now, like a good girl, time's a-wastin'."

Mavis, who only moments before had been singing at the top of her lungs, made no sound at all as a hand reached down to yank at her gaily printed headscarf and use it to drag the lifeless body across the blue and white floor tiles. Mavis's left leg slid limply through a small spill of coffee on one cold square. She had meant to mop the floor the minute she finished the sink and counter. She had thought she had plenty of time, the way people always do when they begin an ordinary day no different from any other.

But Mavis had been wrong.

She hadn't had time, after all.

The hummingbirds' wings fluttered without interruption as they continued their morning feast. In the kitchen, a soft, smooth voice on the radio sang seductively about a lovers' tryst on a stormy summer night.

But this time, the voice sang alone.

The off-key but enthusiastic voice of the middle-aged woman who loved bright colors and bangle bracelets and hoop earrings and hummingbirds and who had never in her life deliberately hurt another human being, had been silenced.

Forever.

Chapter 2

"Well, what I want to know," Sandy Trotter said to Tanner Leo across the table at Vinnie's, "is when you're going to have your first party now that your father has abandoned you and taken off for Hawaii, leaving you in that gorgeous house all by your lonesome."

Tanner winced at the word "abandoned" and self-consciously ran a hand through her long, wind-blown, dark-brown wavy hair. Leave it to Sandy. Her friends all joked that tall, skinny Sandy had never learned to engage her brain before she put her mouth in motion. Impulsive, always in a rush, a little high-strung, she was constantly sticking her foot in her mouth. She'd just done it again. Sandy knew as well as any of Tanner's friends that Tanner's father, the psychiatrist and teacher Dr. Milton Leo, actually *had* walked out on his wife and daughter when Tanner was eight. Knowing that Tanner was still sensitive about it, no one else mentioned it. Trust Sandy to forget and use the word "abandoned."

"Sandy . . ." Jodie Lawson, Tanner's best friend, said in a shocked undertone. Jodie, whose real name was Joellen, was small, thin, and plain, with short brown hair and glasses.

Sandy shrugged. "I repeat, when's the first big bash? I've got a brand-new outfit I'm dying to wear. Tangerine, off-the-shoulder, gorgeous. Come on, Tanner, what are you waiting for? Your father's been gone over an hour already!"

Charlie Cochran squeezed Tanner's hand and said drily, "What are you, Salem's entertainment director, Sandy? Give Tanner time to catch her breath."

Tanner smiled at him gratefully. That was Charlie, her biggest supporter. Always there when she needed him. "Look," she said, "I'd love to have a party, and I will. But I just took my father to the airport this morning, and it feels like he's still *here*. I can almost smell his pipe. Give me a break, okay? Let me get used to the idea that I'm living in that house alone now. Except for Silly, of course. But she's not there at night. I'll have the biggest bash you've ever seen the minute I can't feel his eyes on me watching to make sure I'm folding the towels into thirds instead of halves, and placing the couch pillows facing out instead of sideways, and taking the plants into the kitchen to water them so they don't leave water rings on the hardwood floor in his study."

Jodie, relaxing since Tanner hadn't been offended by Sandy's insensitive comment, laughed. "It's hard to believe your father's a psychiatrist. He's so utterly compulsive! Maybe you should suggest that he see a good therapist."

Everyone laughed, except Tanner. She had given in to her mother's urgings and come to Twin Falls to live with her father in order to get a free education. Besides seeing private patients in town, her father taught at the college, thus his children, meaning Tanner Melissa Leo, could attend Salem University free of charge. She had had no desire to see her father after all these years, much less live with him, but her mother was adamant. "Free is free," she'd said crisply, "and he owes us. I'm off to the Orient for a much-needed and well-deserved vacation, and you're off to Twin Falls, New York, end of conversation." Then she had added ominously, "He's not an easy man to live with. But you're tough. You can take it. And it's only for four years."

Four years!

Tanner had learned quickly how right her mother was. Her father was a stern, unexpressive man who required great peace and order in his life. But Tanner felt no sense of peace in living with him. He was as different from her easygoing, almost sloppy mother as night from day.

Her mother, Gwen Reed (she had dropped the Leo two hours after the divorce, saying she was glad to get rid of it, a statement that had hurt her daughter's feelings, since *her* last name was still Leo) was fond of take-out Chinese, delivery pizza, paper napkins, loud rock music, and men who called her "Babe" but were kind to Tanner, always. Gwen Reed had a tousle of bright red, naturally curly hair, and wore miniskirts, often in black leather, and thigh-high boots. Her voice was as loud as the printed T-shirts she was fond of wearing. She was noisy, messy, fun, and loving — in a brusque, casual sort of way.

After five hours in her father's house, Tanner had trouble imagining her parents ever being together for more than five minutes. Her father wore a suit all day long, even in the evening when he was reading his medical magazines, smoking his pipe, his feet up on a leather hassock at the foot of his recliner, listening to classical music. Rock was expressly forbidden, he made that very clear, his upper lip curling when he said the word "rock." He did *not* watch television, ever, not even the news. There was a small set in the kitchen, but only Silly, the housekeeper, turned it on, watching her beloved soaps in the afternoon when the "perfessor" was out of the house.

Meals in the lovely, ordered house were mostly silent, the cloth napkins folded just so; the tablecloth spotless. At the noisy, haphazard meals in her mother's house, they used cheap place mats on the scuffed wooden table, if they used anything at all. Tablecloths had to be ironed, and if Gwen Reed owned an iron, she kept it well-hidden. Meals were for talking over the day's events, arguing, sometimes even shouting at each other, laughing, listening to music played at full volume. Never a dull moment.

Tanner's father asked her only about her grades, her achievements in her classes, making it clear from the outset that any grade below an A was unacceptable, and then he ate his dinner. Quietly. Not so much as a slurp, a burp, or a hiccough.

And since Tanner had little to say to this man who was virtually a stranger to her, she, too, ate silently.

Their cook and housekeeper, Silly, tried to

help, making small, innocuous comments when she brought another dish into the pretty blue and white dining room, asking Tanner if she'd told her father about the date she had coming up on Saturday night, inquiring of Dr. Leo if he'd shared with his daughter the story about "that patient of yours who jumped off the roof of his garage, and it was in all the newspapers?"

But it was hopeless. Any remarks stimulated by her efforts to help never flowered into actual conversation.

Tanner liked Silly. She was not only a great cook and a meticulous housekeeper (of course, or she wouldn't have lasted a day in that house), she was friendly and funny, providing the lightness and warmth Tanner missed desperately. Without Silly, the house would have been unbearable

She couldn't wait for her father to leave for Hawaii and wished he'd stay for the next three years. The thought of living that long with someone who practically went berserk when the trillions of books on the shelves in his library weren't in alphabetical order according to author made the hairs on the back of her neck rise.

Now, finally, he was gone. And she had the whole, beautiful house to herself. The first thing she was going to do when she got home was scatter the couch pillows every which way and unfold all of the bathroom towels. Then, if lightning didn't strike her, she'd know he really *was* gone, and she'd relax for the first time since she'd arrived at Salem University.

But she wouldn't go near the music room. Tanner shuddered. How she hated that room! Maybe she'd lock it the minute she got home, and give Silly the key for safekeeping until her father got back.

The room was very beautiful. A wide, square space with thick turquoise wall-to-wall carpeting, antique furniture, and a huge stone fireplace. It was filled with half a dozen musical instruments: grand piano, saxophone, violin, cello, trumpet, and a xylophone. Her father played every single one of them, and played them well. Tanner had learned only the violin, a casual admission that had horrified Dr. Leo. "What could your mother have been thinking of?" he had cried, clearly displeased.

Her mother had been thinking of money, that's what her mother had been thinking of, and if he'd been a little more generous with child support, maybe they could have afforded other lessons, other instruments.

Never mind. Tanner wasn't interested in learning to play any other musical instrument, anyway. *He* knew how, so why did anyone else need to?

Besides the musical instruments, which Tanner guessed were the finest made, the shelves along one wall were filled with rare musical manuscripts, carefully wrapped in plastic and clearly labeled.

It should have been a pretty, pleasant place where Tanner could go to relax. But it wasn't.

She wouldn't go into that room while he was gone. Ever.

Her father's parting words to her had been, "Don't forget to practice. You don't want to lose your touch. The key to the music room is on the table in the hall."

Tanner loved playing in the orchestra at Salem and didn't want to lose her touch. But she was *not* going into that room to practice. She never did. Instead, she took her violin up to her lovely, perfectly coordinated bedroom on the second floor and practiced there, knowing it annoyed her father, but not caring.

Vince Kirk strode up to the table, tall, husky, stubborn jaw, sneakers untied, wearing jeans and a gray Salem sweatshirt with tomato sauce slopped down the front in a jagged "Z." Smiling lazily to show he didn't give a fig about the tomato sauce, he slid into the booth, elbowing Jodie aside. "So, your old man's gone, huh?" he said to Tanner. "I thought the air smelled better on campus."

Tanner didn't take offense. Vince had never made any secret of his feelings toward her father. Dr. Leo had given Vince his first-ever F in Psych 101 first semester. Vince showed no signs of forgiveness.

Vince's roommate, Philip Zanuck, arrived right behind him, drinks in hand. Philip was slightly shorter than Vince, but as stocky, with darker hair and a long, serious face. He'd been a big help to Tanner when she first arrived on campus. Philip had taken a summer class at Salem, and knew his way around. She might have dated him eventually, if she hadn't met Charlie Cochran right away.

Philip grinned at Tanner as he slid into the booth. "So, free at last, free at last, eh?"

"You heard."

"Everyone has. The buzz on campus is, Tanner's having a bash. That true?"

Tanner shifted uncomfortably. "Well, sure. Sooner or later."

Philip laughed. "Man, I'd give a lot to see your old man's face if he came home and found that house rocking on its foundation."

"Oh, yeah, me, too," Tanner said drily.

"That'd be a real treat. Of course, I wouldn't be one of the survivors."

Philip was no fan of Dr. Leo's, either. Philip was smart, even brilliant, but her father, who had him in class, told Tanner that Philip's mind was "out in left-field somewhere. That boy's never going to amount to anything if he doesn't get his head out of the clouds and get his act together."

It was true. Philip often seemed distracted, and was constantly losing his keys, his wallet, a paper he'd written. But he was paying his own way through school, working part-time in a garage in Twin Falls, and Tanner thought that should count for something with her father. It didn't seem to.

Tanner never lost her wallet or keys, but, like Philip, she did her share of daydreaming, including fantasizing about having her own room on campus.

They were discussing party plans when a good-looking, expensively dressed boy carrying a plastic bag from a record shop at the mall approached their table. Sloane Currier leaned on the table and said heartily, "Invite me, and my newest CD's are yours for the night."

Tanner didn't laugh. Sloane Currier was *not* one of her favorite people. He had far too much money for his own good and made sure that everyone knew he had it. Sloane was a show-off. He had started school a semester late because he'd been "touring Europe," and loved to brag about it.

Jodie said Sloane was "overcompensating" because he wasn't that great a student. Tanner said that Jodie had taken Psych 101 far too seriously, and that Sloane wasn't overcompensating, he was just conceited.

"I don't even know when I'm having a party," she said coolly in answer to Sloane's offer.

"Man, I can't believe the eminent psychiatrist Dr. Milton Frederick Leo finally blew town," Sloane said, looking directly at Tanner, who felt his gaze on her but refused to meet his eyes. She focused on the white Formica tabletop instead. "I thought Tyrannosaurus rex would never leave. Everyone hear that big sigh of relief on campus?"

Tanner was quickly wearying of hearing her father put down. It was one thing for her to complain about him. She had to live with him. But she felt disloyal listening to everyone else make fun of him. He *was* her father, after all. "My father's no tyrant," she snapped. "He just has high standards."

Sloane hooted derisively.

"We were just discussing party plans," Sandy said, smiling at Sloane, "and we've been ordered to ease off Tanner by her keeper, Charlie Cochran."

"Charlie is not my keeper," Tanner said stiffly. She disengaged her fingers from Charlie's. "I don't *have* a keeper. And *I* make all my decisions, thank you very much. I'll party when I'm good and ready." She grinned as she stood up and slid out of the booth. "Could be any minute now. But first, I have to run over to the library for some quick research and then I have to get home and do some minor rearranging."

"Don't make us wait too long," Sloane said, sliding into the place she'd vacated. "It's been at least a week since my last party and I'm beginning to suffer party withdrawal pangs. So hurry it up, okay, Tanner?"

Tanner dismissed him with a wave of her hand. If she had a party, it would be because *she* wanted to, not because Sloane Currier demanded it.

Charlie walked her to the library. Campus was beautiful at night, Tanner decided, especially in early spring when the trees were bearing newborn leaves of bright green lace. The old-fashioned round globes topping the black iron lamp posts cast a lemon-yellow glow over the rolling lawns, thick and lush now with new growth.

Tanner loved Salem. She loved its wide brick and stone buildings, the carillon at the top of the Tower, the music building, and the library, its shelves overflowing with books. She loved her classes, the parties, the clubs, the dances, the football and basketball games, and the track meets. She loved all of it.

But she never walked across campus without yearning to live in one of the dorms, although none of them was half as impressive-looking as her father's house on Faculty Row. She'd been in some of the dorms. They were noisy and messy and some were very worn, their walls faded, their hardwood floors scuffed. They smelled of basement cafeterias or dining halls, of laundry soap and bleach, of varnish and floor wax. Tanner loved them. They were wonderfully chaotic, with people racing into and out of doors, rushing for the elevator, shouting to one another, playing rock or rap at full volume, borrowing hair dryers and shampoo and towels and sweaters from one another. Messy, noisy, just like her life with her mother. She missed that.

Living with her father was calm and well-ordered and . . . the word that came to mind was "chilly." It was chilly in that house, no matter what the temperature. But it was free, and the dorms weren't, not even for children of faculty. So, no choice there.

Charlie had a fraternity meeting to attend, so he left her on the steps of the library, saying he'd call her later. He kissed her good-bye, although people were running up and down the steps. Shouts of "All right, go to it!" filled the air around them. Charlie and Tanner ignored them and made the kiss a long, meaningful one.

When Charlie turned and loped away, Tanner watched him go. He was one of the good guys. She had dated in high school, including one semi-serious romance, but she'd never met anyone like Charlie. He was funny and sweet, doing old-fashioned things like opening the car door for her and sometimes bringing her a flower when they weren't even going to a dance, just a movie on campus, and calling her every night to tell her to sleep tight. Once, shortly after they'd met, he'd whipped off his windbreaker and tossed it across a puddle at her feet, outside the science building, so she could walk across it without getting wet. People passing by had hooted in derision, and Tanner, laughing, had quickly scooped up the jacket before it was ruined. "It's the thought that counts," she'd said, kissing him on the cheek. "Nice to know that chivalry isn't completely dead."

In spite of his old-fashioned way of treating her, which Charlie said his mother had hammered into him from the time he was born and lay in a crib next to a baby girl, he gave her all the space and freedom she needed. Charlie never tried to make decisions for her, never interfered with her very busy schedule at school, never talked down to her like some guys did to girls. He gave his mother credit for that, too. "Treat a woman well," Charlie quoted, "but if you have to baby her, she's not intelligent enough for you."

Tanner couldn't wait to meet Charlie's mother.

When she had finished at the library, she headed for home. She loved walking alone on campus, and was never nervous. Things happened on campus, she knew that. She'd heard stories. The most frightening had to do with Nightingale Hall, a huge, gloomy, old off-campus dorm down the highway a short distance. Everyone called it *Nightmare* Hall." It sat atop a hill overlooking the road, surrounded by creepy-looking giant trees that cast dark shadows over the worn brick house. Tanner and Jodie couldn't understand why anyone would want to live there, and had decided the cost must be practically nil.

Still, she thought as she approached her father's house on Faculty Row, which was worse? Living in an ugly house like Nightmare Hall with noise and friends and probably a lot of chaos, or living in a beautiful house in chilly silence?

The house really was pretty, she had to admit that. The prettiest house on the street. Situated on a wooded, corner lot on Faculty Row, Dr. Leo's home was a medium-sized, two-story structure built of mellowed antique red brick and trimmed in pristine white. Shiny black shutters framed the windows. The stone walkway leading to the front door was lined with carefully tended beds of early spring flowers. A fat wreath of dried flowers adorned the door and a large red mailbox hung on the wall over the front stoop. Although the upstairs was dark, lights shown from the living room and kitchen windows.

The streetlight on the corner cast a soft, pale glow over the house and its surrounding, perfectly manicured grounds, making the property look warm and welcoming. The surveillance cameras installed to continually scan the front yard were at each end of the roofline, unobtrusively placed so they were barely noticeable.

Perfect, Tanner thought, hesitating at the front gate of the white picket fence surrounding the yard. It just looks so very, very perfect.

So why, she wondered, don't I want to go inside? Why, she wondered, would I rather be anywhere else but here?

Because that was how she felt, standing at the gate. A pulse at her temple had begun to throb, the muscles between her shoulder blades suddenly felt drawn as tightly as her violin strings, and her stomach felt hollow, as if it had a huge, gaping hole in it.

She did *not* want to go inside.

Chapter 3

"What am I doing?" Tanner murmured, pulling the gate open. "He's not *there*! I should be excited about going inside when I know he's miles away. What's wrong with me?" She laughed softly to herself. "Maybe I need a shrink."

Silly would be inside. She didn't leave on Tuesdays until eight, because Dr. Leo had late appointments on that day.

Of course, Tanner thought to herself as she opened the front door, maybe now that the good doctor has taken off for exotic islands, Silly will decide to leave early on Tuesdays. That would be disappointing. It was a lot more fun entering the house to the sound of the housekeeper's voice booming, "Well, hello there, Missy, how was your day? Break any hearts? Got cookies in the oven, out in a minute, you can have a handful and spoil your supper. Then the Doc'll give me that look, the one that's supposed to petrify these old bones. Takes more than a look to scare *me*, I'll tell you. Go ahead, eat up, put some meat on those bones." Then she'd laugh in that raucous, gutsy way that reminded Tanner, with a pang, of her mother's lusty laughter.

But a moment later, as she closed the door behind her, Tanner grimaced in disappointment as she entered a house so still, so quiet, it couldn't possibly have Silly in it. Even if the housekeeper hadn't called out a greeting, there would have been the sound of pans rattling or cookie sheets sliding out of the oven or the clanking of silverware being loaded into the dishwasher. Something, some sound.

There was nothing.

Tanner dropped her pile of books on a small telephone table in the paisley-wallpapered foyer and moved on down the shiny hardwood floor in the hall toward the staircase. Maybe Silly was upstairs, changing the linens, wearing headphones as she listened to her music, forgetting that she could now blast her radio as loud as she wanted to. The master of the house hadn't been gone long enough for Silly to realize how free they were.

Tanner ran lightly up the carpeted stairs, calling, "Silly? Silly, are you here?"

There was no answer.

And although Tanner checked each of the three spacious bedrooms, all immaculate, the beds neatly made as always, no speck of dust anywhere, she saw no sign of the housekeeper.

Tanner stood in the center of her own pale apricot and white bedroom, feeling vaguely disoriented. Also unsettled because she suddenly felt very much alone. She had been so eager for her father to leave, couldn't wait to see his plane take off into the wide blue yonder. Now, here she was, alone at last, and instead of rejoicing, she was feeling blue. What was *that* from? If her father walked in the front door right this very minute, would her heart leap with joy?

Hardly.

It wasn't that he was gone. It was that Silly was, too. Tanner had been looking forward to a nice, cozy dinner at the small, round, wooden table in the kitchen, just the two of them, talking and laughing. She could tell Silly things, things about Charlie and about school, without getting a frown or a clucking of the tongue in response. But so far, there hadn't been much of an opportunity, because her father was usually there. Nobody dampened conversation like he did.

Now, just when they were finally alone and could relax and have a good time, Silly hadn't waited.

Tanner sank down on the white eyelet bedspread. She hadn't expected to have to rattle around in this good-sized house all by herself, not just yet. Not right off the bat like this. In fact, she had thought seriously of asking Silly to stay overnight. Just for a night or two. It wasn't as if Silly had family of her own. She didn't. Her husband had fallen off the railroad bridge behind campus in a drunken stupor years ago, and Silly's two children, she had told Tanner matter-of-factly, lived far away and were ashamed of what their mother did for a living. They never called or wrote except for Christmas cards.

"Course," Silly had added drily, "what I do for a living is what put them two through college so's they can hold *their* heads up, but there's no sense fightin' about it. I've got my friends and my church and a nice, fine life. No complainin' here."

Tanner thought Silly was one of the bravest women she'd ever known. Silly had to be lonely sometimes, whether she was willing to admit it or not, so wouldn't she love to stay here in this nice, big house with someone who liked her and wouldn't give her that look designed to petrify her old bones?

But she'd already left, so she wouldn't be staying on this, the first night of freedom in the Leo house.

Maybe tomorrow night.

Tanner thought briefly about calling the housekeeper to invite her back that night. Her number was on the cork bulletin board beside the refrigerator.

But that would mean another long bus ride. Didn't seem fair.

I could go pick her up, Tanner thought, standing up. Wasn't that why I insisted on taking him to the airport, so that I could have the car while he was gone?

Making up her mind, Tanner ran back down the stairs and into the kitchen. A chocolate layer cake, thickly frosted with more chocolate, slick and shiny as glass, sat on a plate in the center of the wooden table. At least a quarter of it was missing.

That was weird. Silly never ate sweets. She had too much trouble with her teeth. "A few minutes of pleasure," she said, "ain't worth the hours of pain. Or the money. Hardly anything's more costly than a visit to the dentist these days."

Maybe this one time she'd decided the few minutes of pleasure would be worth it. Tanner didn't blame her. Silly's chocolate cakes were out of this world.

Then she saw the note, propped up against the cake plate. Of course. Silly wouldn't take off early without leaving a message of some kind. Usually her notes told what was for dinner and which chores she'd left for Tanner to do. Dr. Leo believed in young adults having responsibility. He said it built character. Then I must have lots of it, Tanner had thought in response. Her mother hadn't been really big on housekeeping and if Tanner hadn't done it, it wouldn't have been done at all.

She did her chores, such as they were, without complaint. The one thing she had insisted upon was that she wasn't dusting the music room. "Afraid I'll break something valuable," she'd confided to Silly, and Silly had grinned and said, "Me, too. But I get paid and you don't, so I'll take the risk. You can unload the dishwasher instead."

I should have looked here in the kitchen first, Tanner told herself, instead of scouring the house for Silly. This kitchen practically belongs to her. Where else would she leave a message?

The note, neatly printed in pencil, read:

Ice cream in freezer. Help yourself. Mavis.

Tanner frowned. Also weird. Nothing about dinner, nothing about leaving early, nothing about baking the cake to celebrate their freedom. They had joked about it, Silly doing a little dance around the kitchen, waving a wooden spoon in the air like a magic wand, saying, "Oh, aren't we just going to have the grandest time, just the two of us, when His Majesty is gone?"

As for the ice cream, Tanner did understand why it was mentioned in the note. Dr. Leo absolutely forbade the confection in his house, saying it was nothing but sugar and air and he expected a "decent" dessert at the end of a meal; that was one of the reasons he paid a cook. Tanner loved ice cream. Silly knew that, and must have made a special trip to the store to buy some, probably the minute Tanner and her father had left the house that morning. What a nice thing to do! She hadn't had ice cream after a meal since she'd left Ashtabula.

That explained Silly telling her about the ice cream. But, the note still seemed unusually cryptic. Tanner sat down in one of the kitchen chairs, studying the piece of paper. Weird that it didn't say what was for dinner.

And Silly had signed the note "Mavis"? Tanner never called her that.

Still, glancing at the cake again, Tanner

guessed what must have happened. Silly had given in to temptation, chowed down on chocolate cake, and before you could say, "Big mistake!" that back tooth that gave her so much trouble had started throbbing and she'd had to rush to get to the dentist before he left for the day. Hadn't even had time to write down tonight's menu.

It didn't matter. There was probably a casserole or some chicken in the oven, and there were always salad fixings in the vegetable drawer of the fridge.

The ice cream in the freezer beckoned, but Tanner decided to be the responsible adult her father was so convinced she wasn't, and eat a decent meal first. Anyway, Silly had made it; it shouldn't go to waste.

When she pocketed the note and stood up, she moved to the refrigerator, anticipating a chilled pasta salad or thick sandwiches on a plate.

But there was no prepared meal on any of the shelves.

Tanner closed the door. No problem. She'd make her own sandwich. Heaven knew she'd been doing it most of her life. Wasn't a bad little cook herself, if the truth were known. But it was so unlike Silly to leave without fixing something. That toothache must have come on before she'd got around to cooking dinner. She'd be apologizing all over the place when she returned. She'd probably cook a bunch of meals at the same time and stick them in the freezer, just in case.

In fact, maybe she'd already done that, sometime before Tanner arrived. There could be all kinds of goodies in that wide, squat freezer on the back porch. Anything in there would thaw quickly in the state-of-the-art microwave beside the stove.

First things first. She'd call Charlie and talk for, oh, maybe an hour now that no one was here to say, "Did you not speak with this person today on campus? What could possibly have happened between then and now that you must discuss at length, I wonder?"

Yes, she would talk for hours, first to Charlie, then to Jodie and Sandy. If she lived on campus in a lovely, noisy dorm, she wouldn't have to spend so much time on the telephone.

She got up from her chair. Her right foot caught on something, almost tripping her. Glancing down, she found an inexpensive fake-leather strap looped around the toe of her black flat. She reached down and tugged gently on the strap.

Attached to it was a purse, brown and worn and overstuffed.

Silly's purse. She only had one. Tanner knew that was so, because no matter what brightly colored, sometimes gaudy, outfit Silly was wearing, she always carried the shabby brown purse. She liked colorful things, and if she had had a bright yellow or red or kelly green purse, she would have carried it.

What was Silly's purse doing under the kitchen table? Had she left in such a rush that she'd forgotten it? Wasn't her bus pass in it? Without that pass, how had she got to the dentist's office?

Maybe the bus driver knew her so well by now that when he'd seen how she was suffering, he'd relented and let her travel for free.

But why hadn't she called by now to make sure her purse was indeed safely at the Leo house? Could she still be at the dentist? Maybe she was home, but her mouth was still numb from novocaine and she couldn't talk.

Tanner went to the cork bulletin board, found Silly's number, and dialed it.

No answer.

Still at the dentist's? After all this time? She had to have left early, since she hadn't had time to fix anything for dinner.

Tanner hesitated. Maybe the number of Silly's dentist was in her purse somewhere. She could call the dentist's office, ask them to tell the housekeeper that her purse was safe, and that if Silly needed it before morning, Tanner would be happy to drop it off once she knew Silly was home. A ride downtown on such a beautiful spring night might be fun. Maybe she'd call Charlie and ask him to join her. It wasn't that late. And it wasn't as if she had to sign in when she came home. That was one nice thing about not living in a dorm.

Feeling a little guilty about invading Silly's private property but telling herself it was necessary, Tanner hunted until she found a small, black telephone notebook. The only doctor was a "Dr. Leidig." Maybe he was the dentist, maybe not. It was worth a try.

She called, aware that it was late in the evening. If they weren't still working on Silly's mouth, no one would be there.

A woman answered on the third ring, saying in answer to Tanner's first question that yes, Dr. Leidig was a dentist. She sounded impatient. They had just finished an emergency procedure, she went on, and she devoutly hoped that Tanner didn't have another one, because she was late getting home as it was.

"No, it's not an emergency," Tanner explained. "But a friend of mine is a patient of

Dr. Leidig's. In fact, I think she's probably there now. I need to tell her that she left her purse at my house."

"You said she," the woman replied. "Our emergency isn't a she. It's a he. Emergency root canal. What's your friend's name? She's not here now, but I can tell you if she came in today."

"Mavis," Tanner said. "Mavis Sills." She smiled to herself. Mavis Sills, who sang country songs at the top of her lungs, baked a fantastic chocolate cake, suffered from bad teeth, and was friendly and funny, bringing warmth into a chilly house. "Mavis Sills," she repeated.

"Oh, yes, Mavis," the woman said. "Don't you just love her? She's such a card! But she hasn't been in today. In fact, if you see her, you might remind her that she's late for her annual checkup." She clucked her tongue in disapproval. "I know she hates to spend the money, but every time she ignores her checkups, she suffers for it. You scold her for me, okay?"

"Sure. I'll do that." Tanner hung up.

She walked back to the table and sat down in a chair again. She picked up the note and studied it, deeply puzzled.

Silly had left early. Hadn't even cooked tonight's dinner, had only taken time to scribble a note about ice cream in the freezer. Had left in such a rush, she'd forgotten her purse. Didn't you have to be in a really terrible rush to forget your purse? *Everything* was in your purse, everything important: keys, change, bus pass, money . . . wouldn't you remember the minute you were outside, on the steps or sidewalk, that you didn't have anything hanging from your shoulder?

Silly had left in a terrible rush.

But she wasn't at her apartment.

And she wasn't at the dentist's office having that bad tooth fixed.

Then . . . where *was* she?

Telling herself that Silly was probably out with friends having a good time (and ignoring a little voice in her head that said, without her *purse*?) Tanner went upstairs to shower.

Fifteen minutes later, comfortable in royal blue sweats and bare feet, she returned to the kitchen. Her stomach was complaining that she should eat before settling down with the telephone. She was so eager for the taste of ice cream that instead of taking the time to thaw and heat something, she tossed together a sandwich and ate it with a handful of chips and a glass of milk.

She was heading for the sink with her plate and glass when she thought she heard something in the hallway, a muffled sound that could have been Silly carefully closing the front door. Returning to collect her purse.

Tanner turned around, glancing up at the small screen high on the kitchen wall reflecting the view from the cameras outside. The screens were in every room except her bedroom. She saw nothing but the front yard, the picket fence, and the walkway to the front door. "Silly? Is that you?"

No husky, hearty voice responded with a cheerful, "Yeah, it's me, forgot my purse. I'd forget my head if it wasn't screwed on." There was no answer at all from the darkened hallway.

Disappointed, Tanner swiveled back to the sink.

She rinsed her dishes, and was bending to stash them in the dishwasher when she heard another sound, this one louder than the first. This one was an "oof" sound, as if someone had bumped into something, possibly the small telephone table in the hall.

Silly wouldn't have bumped into anything. She knew this house like the back of her hand.

"Silly?" Tanner said again, her hands pausing in their task. No answer. Her heart began to pound in her chest. She *had* locked the front door, hadn't she? "Silly?"

"If there's one thing I'm not," a voice said from behind her, "it's silly." Then, before Tanner could turn around, something as hard as a rock slammed against the back of her skull. She felt no pain at all, nothing but a numbing disbelief that swept over her like a dark curtain. Then her eyes closed and she toppled forward, crumpling onto the open dishwasher.

Chapter 4

When Tanner came to, the first thing she became conscious of was the quiet. She had never heard such quiet. There wasn't a sound. No ordinary indoor sounds, like voices from a television or music from a radio or footsteps tapping across a hardwood floor or the metallic "pop" of a can of soda being opened in the kitchen. No outside sounds, like the chirping of tree frogs or the rumbling of car engines, no dogs barking, no doors slamming as people arrived home, no lawnmowers, no birds singing, no distant train whistle.

Quiet. The air was full of it, as thick as the frosting on Silly's cake.

Silly. Where *was* she? Why wasn't she here, where she was supposed to be, when Tanner needed her?

The sharp irritation she felt toward Silly brought Tanner all the way back to consciousness. She lifted her head, opened her eyes.

Her heart sank as she realized where she was. In the music room. That explained the silence. The entire room was completely sound-proof. No sound at all entered or exited. She had hated that about the room on the one occasion when she'd been in it. She had been alone then, and the feeling of isolation had been almost unbearable.

A second wave of distress hit her as she remembered. She wasn't alone now. She'd been in the kitchen and someone had come up behind her and hit her. Panic brought Tanner upright, her eyes wide with alarm.

He was sitting opposite her, lounging casually on the blue pin-dotted sofa, legs up, feet resting on one arm of the sofa. Green plaid flannel shirt. Khaki pants, seriously wrinkled, inkstains on one pocket. She couldn't see his face.

She couldn't see his face because it was completely hidden behind a grotesque rubber Halloween mask of an old, old man, the skin gray and wrinkled, the brows frowning furiously, the nose hawkish, the mouth cut thin and mean and narrow. A cheap wig made of tufts of white hair covered his own hair.

Fury flooded Tanner. Coward! Hiding behind a mask! But then, what did she expect from a thief? Weren't they all cowards, sneaking into people's homes to skulk off with whatever valuables they could get their hands on?

She had no idea what she was supposed to do. She had never, not once in her life, imagined someone intruding into the privacy of her own home, wherever that might be. Their neighborhood in Ashtabula hadn't been the best, but even in an area as modest as theirs, they'd felt safe. At least, she had. She had never thought seriously about how she would behave if something this horrible should happen.

She struggled to gather her chaotic thoughts together. Maybe thieves were like dogs. Maybe they smelled fear, and it made them attack.

She would hide her fear. Try, anyway. Give it her best shot. She had to do *something*.

The telephone rang.

"Ignore it," he said coolly, rubbery lips moving.

"My friends know I'm here," she said shakily. "They'll think it's weird if I don't answer."

"No, they won't. They'll think you're in the shower. Don't sweat it. Relax."

Oh, right. That should be no problem. Didn't she have thieves in her house just about every night? No biggie.

"What do you want?" she said coldly, marveling at the sudden, surprising control in her voice. "What are you doing here?"

"Just relaxing. This is a very comfortable couch, by the way. And I'm trying to do some thinking here, so would you please just shut up? I'll tell you when you can talk."

Tanner's jaw dropped. This is *my* house! she felt like shouting. But she didn't. He had hit her on the head. He was dangerous.

The telephone rang again. He waved a hand in dismissal and although every nerve in her body shrieked at her to snatch up the receiver and scream into it, she didn't dare. Her screams would summon help, but what would he do to her in the meantime? Help would arrive too late.

Don't be so melodramatic, she told herself to calm down her singing nerves. He's a thief, not a killer.

But he'd already knocked her out once, her aching head reminded her, and she didn't want another blow. It hurt. Maybe he wasn't a killer, but it obviously didn't bother him to inflict pain. She didn't want any more of that, if she could help it.

"Just take what you want and get out," she said, leaning forward slightly, her voice intense. "Please. Just go."

He turned his head to look at her through the narrow little eye slits in the rubber mask. "Go? You want me to go already? I just got here!" He shrugged and returned his gaze to the huge, stone fireplace. "You're not much of a hostess. Now, shut up while I think."

Frustrated and confused, Tanner gave up, sinking back into the black leather chair. Her father's chair. This was where he sat every evening, reading the newspaper, smoking his pipe. He had never invited her to join him, but she wouldn't have, anyway. Not in this room.

The musical instruments, all six of them, were worth a lot of money. Also the rare manuscripts on the shelves. Was that why the intruder was here? If he was, why didn't he just take them and go? She couldn't stop him. He was bigger than she was.

It really was a pretty room, she thought dispassionately. The turquoise carpeting was thick and expensive, and the furniture was nicer than anything they'd had in Ohio. But what she hated most about the room was that it was soundproof. Her father had said, "Well, of course it is," making Tanner feel stupid. It made her skin crawl, knowing that when she was inside, no one beyond the four walls could hear a sound she made. The sense of unreality that came over her in the soundless room reminded her of a question her father had slyly asked her at dinner one night: "If a tree falls in the forest and no one is there to hear it, does it make any sound?" When Tanner went into the music room that first time, she had thought, *If no one in this world can hear me right now, how do I know I really exist?*

It wasn't only the soundproofing that made the room seem so isolated. In order to keep damaging light and dust off the instruments and manuscripts, all four of the room's windows were set high up in the wall, almost to the ceiling. There was no way to see out, and no way for anyone to see in. It was as if the outside world had been sucked up into a giant vacuum.

Thanks to a skylight in the roof, the space was bright, and should have been cheerful. But it didn't seem so to Tanner. It seemed to her that a graveyard, with the sounds of birds singing and traffic passing by and the smells of fresh-mowed grass and spring flowers, would feel more alive than this room.

She didn't want to be here.

"Will you *please* just take what you want and get out?" she cried. "I hate this room, and I want out of here!"

His head snapped around. He jumped up off the couch and strode, in two steps, to stand before her. "I didn't come here to *take* anything!" he shouted. "Not some stupid musical instruments and manuscripts, anyway."

It took a few seconds for the remarks to register. When they had, Tanner looked up into the grotesque rubber mask, confusion on her face. "You didn't come to steal anything?" The confusion was quickly replaced by uneasiness. "I don't understand. Then . . . then why *are* you here?"

He threw his head back and laughed, a crude, harsh sound that seemed to insult the peaceful silence of the room. "The daughter of the prominent psychiatrist doesn't comprehend?" He crouched in front of her, the mask so close to her face she could have reached out and ripped it off his head if she'd dared. She didn't.

"Let me explain," he said slowly, patiently. "I am not going anywhere just yet. And *you* are not going anywhere any time soon." He stood up. "This," he said, waving his hands to encompass the entire room, "is where you are going to be living from this moment on. In this one room. And it's not such a bad room, is it? I've seen worse. Oh, yes, I have certainly seen worse."

While she stared up at him, totally bewildered, he fished in his back pocket and withdrew something. He held it up in front of her, letting it dangle tantalizingly close. A key. The key, she knew immediately, to the music room. It was in his possession now, and he wanted her to know it.

He had locked them in.

Why?

He left her then, got up and went back over to flop down on the couch again. He began talking, lazily, casually, staring up at the ceiling as he spoke. But his words, Tanner realized with growing horror, were anything but casual.

"You're not going to leave this room," he said. "This is where you're going to spend your days. And your nights. You're going to sleep in here, and eat in here, when I feel like bringing you some food." He spread his hands again. "This is your room now, Tanner. So it's really too bad that you hate it. Personally, I think it's very nice. Lots of space for you to move around in. You're luckier than some, if you ask me."

Tanner had been stricken speechless. She sat forward in the chair, her fists clenched, trying desperately to digest what he was saying. She was to stay? In here? In this room? Eat here, sleep here, spend her days here? No, that couldn't be, it had to be a joke of some kind. A joke would explain the stupid mask. Her friends knew how she felt about this room. Had they gotten together and decided to play a little prank on her to celebrate her father's trip?

One hand went to the back of her head, where a dull ache had begun to throb mercilessly. No. No, her friends would never let anyone hurt her like this. Never. Charlie wouldn't. Charlie would jump in front of a speeding car headed in her direction. He would certainly never give anyone permission to hammer on her skull.

This was no prank.

"You can't keep me in here," she said slowly, carefully. "That's . . . that's ridiculous. That's kidnapping! Keeping me a prisoner in my own house? That's the craziest thing I've ever heard!"

The masked head turned toward her, the gray rubber "skin" around the mouth creased, and although Tanner couldn't actually see the smile, she could feel it. "Actually, you're wrong," he said. "It's not at all ridiculous. I think it's close to brilliant. And it was really thoughtful of your father to have this room soundproofed. Perfect. Absolutely perfect!"

Tanner sat very still. He meant it. He meant to keep her there, in this room. For how long? Days, at least, he had said. Days? *Days?*

This couldn't be happening. How had he gotten in? Had she forgotten to lock the front door?

She sometimes did. But Faculty Row, with its lovely, big, white houses and neat yards and respectable professors behind the closed doors, had always seemed perfectly safe. Forgetting to lock the front door hadn't seemed like a dangerous oversight. Until now.

Tanner glanced around her. There was only one door in and out of the room, and the key to that door was in his possession. She would never be able to get it away from him. His shoulders were twice the size of hers. The only other door led to a tiny lavatory. But it had no outside door and no windows.

"You're going to keep me a prisoner in here?" she asked when she found her voice again. "Why? Why would you do something so crazy? My father doesn't have enough money to pay any ransom."

"Oh, for pete's sake, *you're* not worth anything!" he said, his words heavy with contempt. "The instruments and the manuscripts are worth a hundred times *your* value."

"Then *what*?" Tanner shouted. "What do you *want*?"

"Satisfaction," he said clearly. "Satisfaction." And began humming the melody to the Rolling Stones tune, "I Can't Get No Satisfaction."

His obvious calm when *she* felt as if she had

fireworks going off in her stomach was maddening. "Well, I'm *not* staying in this room with you!" she cried, even though it was becoming increasingly clear that she wasn't being given any choice in the matter. "I'm not!"

"Oh, *I'm* not staying," he said nonchalantly, sitting up and facing her. "Nope, not me. I have places to go, things to do, people to see. But you, you're not going anywhere. Of course, I'll be back. Just can't say when, that's all. Maybe tomorrow, maybe not until Thursday. I have a very busy schedule."

The news that he wouldn't be staying was a massive relief to Tanner. Maybe, when he left, she could figure out some way to escape. Yes, of course she could. There had to be a way. It was just too ridiculous to believe that she could be kept a prisoner in her father's music room. Crazy. *Insane.*

"What if I get hungry?" she asked as he got up and moved toward the door.

"Then you get hungry," he said, shrugging. "Tough. Maybe it's time for you to learn that you don't always get what you want when you want it. A very valuable lesson, one I learned a while ago. If I remember, I'll bring you something to eat when I come back. *If* I remember," he added cruelly. "I've got a lot on my mind these days." He bent to unplug the telephone from the wall, wrapped the cord around it and cradled it under his arm.

She hadn't thought for a second that he would be dumb enough to leave the telephone, but seeing it in his possession, knowing he was about to walk out of the room with her only means of communication under his arm, made her headache worse.

"You can't just leave me here like this," she said. "It's . . . it's stupid! Anyway, my friends will come looking for me."

"Well, we're going to take care of that little detail right now." He pulled a sheet of paper and a pen from his pocket. Handing both items to her, he said, "Write what I tell you."

"No." Tanner curled her hands into small fists. "I'm not writing anything."

"Yes, you *are*." He dropped the pen and paper in her lap. His voice hardened as he added, "And you'd better start realizing who's in charge here, miss, if you know what's good for you." He grabbed a handful of her hair and yanked, hard. "Now write!"

Tanner picked up the paper and pen and wrote as he dictated.

I'm not going to stay in this house alone. I've gone to join my mother in the Orient. Sorry, Charlie, but I know you'll under-

stand. I'll send you all postcards. See you next fall!

Love,
Tanner

"My friends will never believe that I'd just take off without calling them to say good-bye," Tanner said stubbornly. "And this note makes it sound like I was afraid to stay here alone. They won't buy that, either. They know how much I was looking forward to it. I just talked to them a little while ago about having a party."

"They'll believe it when you don't show up for class and you don't call them. I'm going to hang this note on the mailbox. They'll see it when they come looking for you. Even if they should get suspicious and go to the police, this note is in your handwriting. You're all grown up and can go wherever you want. The police will think that you left of your own free will, and no one knows how to get in touch with your old lady to check things out, so . . ."

"How do you know that?" Tanner regarded the ugly mask suspiciously. "And how did you know this room was soundproof? How do you know so much about me and my family?"

The head tilted slightly. "Oh, didn't I mention that I know your father? Pretty well, in fact. To know the man is to love him. *Not.*"

"You know my father? That doesn't tell me anything. Lots of people know my father. And if you're mad at him, why are you punishing *me*? I didn't do anything to you."

"You ask too many questions. And look, when I come back," he added sternly, "I expect this place to be shipshape. Keep it neat and orderly, hear? That's the way the doc likes it."

It was when he said "neat and orderly" that Tanner remembered Silly. Of course! Okay, so it looked like Tanner Melissa Leo was going to have to spend one very long night locked in this room. But, come morning, Silly would be here, bright and early, letting herself in with her own key, and Tanner would hear her coming in and yell . . .

Well, no, that wouldn't work. Because in *this* room, she wouldn't hear or be heard.

But, thanks to the surveillance cameras, the result of her father's rampant paranoia, she'd be able to see Silly coming in. At least she'd know there was someone else in the house. And even if she couldn't make the housekeeper hear her, sooner or later Silly would tackle the music room as part of her daily chores.

Tanner breathed an inner sigh of relief. She could put up with one night in this place. It would be horrible, but she could do it. And tomorrow, Silly would set her free.

And then it was straight to the police, first thing, no question about that. This guy, whoever he was, couldn't be allowed to run around loose. He was dangerous.

He opened the door. "Oh, by the way," he said cheerfully, "don't expect your house-keeper to show up tomorrow morning. She had a little accident today and won't be in for a while. You'll have to keep this place neat all by your little lonesome. See that you do."

And as Tanner stared after him, open-mouthed, he left, closing the door after him.

A second later, she heard the key turn in the lock.

Chapter 5

When the telephone rang in the small, cluttered room at Lester dorm shared by Jodie Lawson and Sandy Trotter, both girls were lying on their beds, reading. Jodie grabbed for the phone first. She'd been hoping for a call from Luke Hopper, a very interesting-looking guy in her chem class.

The voice did belong to a guy, but it wasn't Luke. "Oh, it's you, Charlie," Jodie said, thin shoulders in flannel pajamas slumping in disappointment. "What's up? Tanner's not here, if that's why you're calling."

Sandy listened with mild curiosity as her roommate, glasses resting on her short, slightly turned-up nose, talked to Tanner's boyfriend. Charlie, a leader on campus, often called to make plans for some event or outing. Sandy, who hated to sit still for more than five minutes, was always interested in something new and different to do.

But this conversation didn't sound like planning.

"Well, she's not here," Jodie repeated, sitting back down on her bed, pajama-clad legs crossed. "I thought she was going to the library."

They talked a few minutes more, then Jodie replaced the receiver. She turned to face Sandy, her hazel eyes concerned. "Charlie says he's been calling Tanner all night and she's not answering."

"Maybe she just didn't hear the phone. She could be in that stupid music room, practicing. She said you can't hear a thing when you're in there. It's soundproof."

"She hates that room. She'd never go in there. Besides, there's a phone in there, I've seen it."

"Is Charlie worried?" Sandy began brushing her hair. It was long, blonde, and very straight. She constantly twirled strands of it around a finger, a nervous habit. "I know they talk every night before they go to bed. Can't he miss one night? It won't kill him, will it? It's not like he won't see her first thing in the morning." A faint note of envy slipped into her words. Sandy dated a lot, but so far, that one great romance had passed her by. She wanted what Charlie and Tanner had. Everyone on campus knew what a great thing they had going. They'd all seen it. And Sandy wasn't the only one envious of their happiness.

"That's not the point, Sandy. What Charlie wants to know is *why* Tanner isn't answering the phone." Jodie thought for a minute, swinging her legs against the bed. "I guess she could be in the shower. I just hope she calls him the minute she's out, or he'll never sleep tonight." She looked at Sandy doubtfully. "So, do you think we should do something? I mean, we could get dressed and run on over to Tanner's, make sure she's okay."

"Of course she's okay." The thought of getting dressed at this hour, maybe even having to go out without makeup on because putting it on would take too much time and Jodie would have a fit, annoyed Sandy. "When is Tanner ever not okay? I mean, the way she talks, she practically raised herself after her father left to come here. Her mother wasn't exactly Mary Poppins, from the sound of things. Tanner can take care of herself. And I need to get some sleep."

Jodie glared at her. "How can you be so sure that Tanner's okay?"

Sandy shrugged. "She just always is, that's

all. Night." And she rolled over on her side, tugging the blankets up over her shoulders.

At the Sigma Chi house, Charlie Cochran wasn't sleeping. He was sitting at his desk, his hand on the telephone. He had called every friend of Tanner's that he knew, and none of them had seen or heard from her. Then he had called her house again, repeatedly. He let the phone ring dozens of times, but there was no answer.

It was nearly midnight. Tanner wasn't with Jodie and Sandy, her best friends. And she certainly wasn't with her boyfriend.

So where *was* she?

Her father was off to Hawaii. The housekeeper, Silly, would have gone home long ago. Which left Tanner in that house alone.

Charlie sat in his desk chair, staring at the shiny hardwood floor. He had nervously run his hands through his dark, shaggy hair so many times, it was standing on end. His roommate was asleep, and the house on a Tuesday night was fairly quiet, so he had no trouble concentrating. But he didn't know what to do.

The uneasiness Charlie felt was new to him. Charlie Cochran didn't *get* uneasy. He had four brothers and had grown up rough and rowdy, learning quickly to take whatever came his way and either bend with it or fight back. It took a lot to knock Charlie's solid underpinnings from beneath him.

His feelings for Tanner had almost done just that. Like her, he had dated a lot in high school, but also like her, had never had really strong feelings for any one person. Until he'd walked into the rec center at Lester one day shortly before Christmas and seen a tall, slim girl with long, dark, wavy hair standing in front of the jukebox pondering the selections. She had the prettiest face he had ever seen, and when she looked up and smiled at Philip, standing opposite her, Charlie felt as if someone had just turned on a dozen strobe lights. Corny, he knew, but everything about that night was incredibly corny.

Charlie had asked her to dance.

She had smiled that wonderful smile and said, "Sure, I'd love to."

They'd been together ever since.

Charlie stood up. He couldn't go to sleep without talking to her. Couldn't. Didn't even want to try.

He grabbed his windbreaker and left the room.

Chapter 6

Tanner sat frozen in the black leather chair for long minutes after the door to the music room had been closed and locked. Unable to hear the sound of the front or back doors closing, she couldn't be sure he'd really gone. Then she remembered the cameras.

Her head shot up, her eyes darting toward the screens high on the wall, one in each of two corners. The screen on the left showed a view of the front of the house, the screen on the right a view of the backyard. But she had waited too long. There was nothing there now but the empty front walkway, the yard, and a deserted Faculty Row. In the backyard, she saw only shrubbery, flowerbeds, the gazebo and the garden benches and trees.

If he really had left the house, she'd missed his departure.

She would have to remember the screens. If

nothing else, she could at least see what was going on outside.

She stood up, her knees shaky. Looked around her. Nothing had changed, nothing looked any different than it had the first time she'd been in this room, except that the pillows on the couch were wrinkled from him. Him! Who was he? Someone her father knew. But her father knew everyone on campus and a lot of people in Twin Falls. The intruder could be anyone. His voice hadn't sounded familiar, although he could have been disguising it. But she was sure she didn't know anyone who could be so cruel, so horrible, so vicious.

But if he wasn't someone she knew, why did he have to be disguised?

Tanner began walking nervously around the perimeter of the room, lost in confused thought. How had this happened? She had gone to the library, Charlie had walked with her, they'd kissed on the front steps, she'd gone inside and done her research, then she'd come home. She could remember now how contented she had felt, walking across campus in the dark, anticipating arriving home to no Dr. Milton Leo anywhere in sight, only Silly and a warm dinner.

Silly. An accident, the intruder had said. What kind of accident? And how did he know?

Tanner's heart rolled over in fear. Was Silly all right? He hadn't hurt her, had he?

She had to get out of this room and find out if Silly was all right.

Tanner glanced up at the windows. Miles above her. Miles and miles, way up there close to the ceiling. No one passing by could see her, nor could she pound on the panes and shout to attract someone's attention. Impossible. The windows were of no use at all.

She went, then, to the heavy wooden door. Rattled the brass knob, pulled, tugged on it, but it was no use. The rest of the house was definitely locked away from her. Frustrated and frightened at the thought of spending an entire night in this room that she hated so, she delivered a vicious kick to the door, forgetting that she was in her bare feet. All that did was send a shaft of pain up her leg.

Limping slightly, she returned to the leather chair and sank down into its cool, slick folds.

"I don't know what to do," she said aloud. "I Do Not Know What To Do."

Was he really going to keep her imprisoned in this room? There was nothing to eat in here, nothing to drink, although there was a tiny sink in the lavatory where she could at least scoop a handful of water from beneath the faucet. She had only had a sandwich and chips for dinner.

She'd be hungry soon. The thought of not being able to meander into the kitchen and fix whatever she pleased, whenever she pleased, began to sink in.

When she became hungry, she couldn't go to the kitchen and grab something to eat.

Her bare feet were cold, but she couldn't run up to her bedroom and grab a pair of warm socks.

She couldn't go into the bathroom down the hall from her bedroom and brush her teeth or wash her face.

She couldn't go anywhere, and she couldn't call anyone to come and let her out, because *he* had taken the telephone when he left.

It was very, very dark outside. Only a tiny glimmer of pale yellow from the corner street lamp was reflected in the skylight and windows.

Tanner got up and turned on another lamp. Then another, until all three of the small desk lamps on the end tables and her father's desk were glowing.

It didn't help.

She walked over to the fireplace. It was no longer used. There was no burned ash lying on the clean white stone. Her father had said, "The smoke would be harmful to the instruments" and she'd had to bite her tongue to keep from replying, "Then why have a fireplace in here?" She had decided the room hadn't always been a music room, hadn't always been sound-proofed, had perhaps at one time been some nice family's living room, a room filled with laughter and light and a roaring fire blazing in the fireplace, with windows placed at normal heights to look out upon the world and let the world look right back in.

To the left of the fireplace was a large wood-box with a hinged lid. Tanner lifted the lid. No wood inside, of course. Why have wood for a fireplace you're never going to use?

She could have used a heavy log as a weapon, waiting behind the door with it in hand until he returned and then slamming it against his head as he entered. Right now, that kind of action seemed like her only hope. But . . . there was no wood, and she didn't see anything else in the room to use as a weapon.

The lid dropped with a thunk that startled her in the deafening silence of the room.

She had just turned away from the woodbox when a movement on one of the square, grayish screens above her head caught her attention. The picture was so small, she had to squint to see clearly.

And her heart leaped for joy. Charlie! Hurrying up the front walk! At this hour?

Of course. They hadn't had their good night talk. They had agreed that they couldn't sleep until they'd told each other good night. And tonight, the intruder had prevented her from having that ritual conversation with Charlie. He must have called, probably more than once. She hadn't heard the phone ring, and couldn't have answered even if she had heard it.

So he'd become worried. He knew she was there alone. He must be frantic, wondering why she hadn't answered the phone.

Tanner ran to the door, whispering, "Charlie, Charlie, you're such a good guy! You're the best, Charlie!" She raised both hands, curled into fists, and began pounding with all of her strength. She kicked, too, first with one foot, then the other, anything to make noise, anything to break the awful silence and tell Charlie she was in the house, yes, she was, she was here, all he had to do was come in and get her.

"Charlie!" she screamed, "Charlie, I'm in here, in the music room!"

Continuing to pound and kick and shout, she turned her head sideways, glanced up at the camera, and saw Charlie reading the note the intruder had pinned to the mailbox. *Her* note, saying she was leaving to join her mother.

It *wasn't* her note. She hadn't written it willingly. But would Charlie know that?

Tanner stopped shouting, stopped pounding and kicking, and stood very still, her eyes on Charlie in the tiny screen. He looked like a miniature person and in the grayness of the screen, his wonderful dark eyes that she loved seemed colorless.

"I didn't write that, Charlie," she muttered from between teeth clenched with tension. "You have to know I didn't write that."

He must have read it a trillion times, it seemed to her. Just kept reading it over and over, didn't even shake his head, just kept his eyes on that piece of paper, clearly unable to comprehend the words.

"I don't blame you, Charlie," Tanner whispered, watching, holding her breath. "You just can't believe that I would take off for Hong Kong or Japan or wherever without calling you first, and you're right, I never would, never! So *think* about that, Charlie! Ask yourself *why* that note supposedly from me would be there when I would never do something so stupid."

Finally, Charlie did shake his head. He pulled the collar of his leather bomber jacket higher up around his chin, and gave his head another shake. He looked down at the note in his hands again. Looked up, at the front door, as if he expected it to open at any second and

Tanner would be standing there, laughing and saying, "Gotcha!" Looked down at the note again. Began to turn slightly sideways . . .

"No!" Tanner screamed at the top of her lungs, "No, Charlie, you can't leave! Wait, don't go! Oh, God, please don't go! I don't want to stay here alone. Please, Charlie, *think* about the note! It's not true, you *know* it can't be true, because I would never go and leave you without calling, I wouldn't, you *know* that!"

But as she stood there screaming, frantically waving arms at him that she knew he couldn't see, he continued to turn away from the door. Then, still holding the note, he took a step forward, away from the house, then another and another.

"No, Charlie, don't, don't go!" Tanner screamed, tears of frustration gathering in her eyes. "I'm here, I'm *here*, Charlie, oh, God, why can't you *hear* me?"

Charlie stopped, and for just one breath of a second, Tanner thought he might somehow have heard her. But instead of turning around, he began walking again.

And although Tanner continued to shout as loud as she could, jumping up and down and waving her arms frantically, begging Charlie to wait, he continued on down the walkway until he was out of camera range and had disappeared from sight.

With a loud, pained wail of defeat, Tanner sank to her knees on the soft, thick, turquoise carpet.

Chapter 7

Tanner didn't kneel on the carpet for long. The image of herself, crouching on the floor in tears, revolted her. And she couldn't stand the thought that the intruder might return at any moment and find her in such bad shape. Whatever it was he was looking for with this crazy plan . . . satisfaction, he'd said, whatever that meant . . . she wasn't about to give it to him so soon, like an early birthday present.

She stood up, wiping her eyes on a bedraggled tissue she unearthed from the pocket of her sweatpants. Glancing at the German cuckoo clock above the fireplace, she saw with dismay that it was only one A.M.! Hours yet to get through before morning arrived. Hours!

Oh, Charlie, why didn't you *hear* me? she cried silently.

The room had grown colder, and her bare feet felt as if she were standing on the frozen pond behind campus. She went into the tiny powder room, hoping for a nice, warm towel, but there were none. Only a handful of crisp paper towels, too small and stiff to substitute for socks.

She cupped her hands under the faucet in the tiny sink, temporarily quenching her thirst. "I would kill for a toothbrush," she said aloud, but had to settle for scrubbing her teeth with a dampened finger. A sound like distant thunder from her stomach reminded her that she was hungry, but the kitchen might as well have been a thousand miles away for all the good it did her.

When she left the powder room, she told herself that the best way to make the night pass quickly was through sleep. If she lay down on the couch and closed her eyes, when she opened them again, it would be morning. Morning would surely bring help of some kind. Maybe the intruder had lied, and Silly was fine. She'd show up, bright and brash as always, and sooner or later, she'd discover Tanner locked in the music room and let her out.

And if Silly *wasn't* all right, if she really had had some kind of accident and didn't show up at all, Charlie, at least, would be back. Charlie wouldn't believe that note, not after he'd thought about it. He'd come back. He *would*.

If she wasn't sure of anything else in the world, she was sure of that much.

Tanner lay down on the couch, but sleep was impossible. She kept listening for the sound of a key in the lock, telling her *he* had returned. She was cold, very cold. There was nothing in the room to use as a blanket. Her feet were like ice, even when she stretched the legs of her sweats down over her toes and tucked her feet underneath her. Unable to sleep, she was forced to think about her situation. Unreal, bizarre, but there it was. Time to face it.

She was locked in a soundproof room. No food. Nothing to keep her warm as the night grew colder. Shouts for help wouldn't do any good, and she couldn't reach the windows to pound on them to attract the attention of a passerby. No telephone. No housekeeper. No father, no mom, no hope of getting out of here on her own . . .

Tears of self-pity and fear stung Tanner's eyelids.

No, dammit! If her crazy captor ever did come back, he wasn't going to find her with tear-swollen eyes. No way.

She curled up into an armadillo-like ball on the narrow couch, and forced her eyelids shut.

Fear and emotional exhaustion finally took their toll and by thinking about Charlie, which comforted her, Tanner managed to doze fit-fully.

The cuckoo had just struck the hour of six, semi-waking her, when the sound of the music room door being unlocked brought her fully back to consciousness. The skylight overhead revealed a dove-gray dawn. The room was as cold as a tomb. Shivering, hugging her arms around her chest for warmth, Tanner sat upright, her fear-widened eyes on the door.

The ugly gray mask peered inside. "Rise and shine!" he said. "Sleep well?"

"I slept fine," she said defiantly. But she couldn't stop shivering with cold. And fear, she had to admit. Her spine crawled at the sight of the repulsive rubber mask peering in at her.

"What's the matter," he said as he entered the room, "you didn't find all the comforts of home in here? Such a nice room. I guess it is a little chilly, though. Too bad." He walked over to her and bent down, the grotesque rubber mask only inches from her face. "You're not going to catch a cold, are you? That's not part of my plan. Maybe I can dig up a blanket for you tonight. Can't have you getting sick on me."

I'm not going to *be* here tonight, Tanner thought vehemently. I'm not spending another horrible night in this room.

He had left the door ajar. But when her eyes swung over to it, so did his. He laughed. "Go ahead, give it a shot," he challenged her. He straightened up to stand over her ominously. "Two bits I get there before you do. And then I'll have to punish you for trying to get away."

Giving up, Tanner sank back into the couch.

He laughed again. Then casually, like someone out taking a leisurely stroll, he sauntered over to the door and reached out into the hall, retrieving with one hand a long, narrow board and pulling it into the room. Dropping it on the floor at Tanner's feet, he moved back to the door to haul in a second board. Then moving quickly back and forth from the doorway to the hall, he brought more boards into the room and piled them atop the others, until several stacks of boards crisscrossed the turquoise carpet.

The last load of boards he brought into the room was made up of shorter pieces of wood. These he piled on the leather chair.

The last thing he lifted into the room and deposited on the floor was a red metal tool kit. Then he closed and locked the music room door again.

Tanner watched the door swing shut with a sickening sense of hopelessness.

Bending to open the lid of the tool kit, he took from it a large claw hammer and a plastic box. "Nails," he said, waving the box at Tanner, who hadn't moved from the couch. "Can't put wood together without nails, right?"

"What are you doing?" she asked, keeping her eyes on him. There hadn't been one single moment when she could have made it through that doorway. He'd been right there the whole time, gathering in his pile of boards. "What is all that lumber for?" When she first saw what he was hauling inside, she'd thought he might be planning to build a fire in the fireplace to warm the room. But the boards were too big. Much too long. Taller than he was.

"None of your business," he said harshly, lifting one board and dragging it over into the middle of the room. Then he went back and got a second one.

She watched as he nailed the two boards together, and then nailed a third and fourth to the first two. He was fast and efficient, wielding the claw hammer as if it weighed no more than an ounce or two. He set aside the first section, which was no wider than the music room door, and began nailing another group of boards together.

"What are you *doing*?" Tanner cried again, when he had two narrow "walls" fastened together, had set them aside, and was beginning a third. "What *is* that?"

"You'll see," he said grimly, and continued pounding.

Tanner suddenly wasn't at all sure she *wanted* Silly to show up. *He* wouldn't like the interruption, and that claw hammer looked like it would make a nasty but very effective weapon. It wasn't as if he'd never hit anyone on the head before. Tanner closed her eyes in pain at the thought of Silly being attacked, and had to quickly tell herself that her imagination was working overtime. Nothing like that could happen. It was too horrible.

But what was he *doing*?

"I'm hungry," she said, hoping to distract him. He was working on a fourth section of boards. "I need something to eat. You said you didn't want me to get sick. If you don't feed me, I will get sick."

He continued to pound nails into the boards. "Later. Shut up."

Tanner sank back against the couch, trying to think. If he went out to the kitchen to get her something to eat, maybe he'd leave the hammer behind, and she could get her hands on it.

But, she thought dismally, he'd never be that careless.

The four sections were completed, lying in wait on the floor. Holding half a dozen long, heavy nails at a time between the lips of the rubber mask, he left one section lying on the floor while he attached one section at each side, creating a lidless "box." Then, with the "box" still lying on its back, he moved a handful of shorter boards from the leather chair to the floor and used them to seal first one end of the "box" and then the other.

It was such a bizarre sight, the figure in the green plaid flannel shirt wearing the gray, wrinkled, rubber mask, nails between its lips, the clumps of white hair bobbing as he hammered away, connecting the walls to each other, like someone fitting together the pieces of a giant jigsaw puzzle.

She would never be able to describe this scene to anyone and expect them to believe it.

Tanner watched intently. A box? He was making a box?

She stopped breathing. A box . . . if it had had a lid, it would have looked exactly like . . .

A coffin.

No. *No!*

Tanner's heart felt as if it were sheathed in ice, and her hands were so stiff she couldn't flex her fingers.

Even when he stood the box upright, it still looked like a coffin.

She didn't want to think about why he would be constructing a coffin.

While she continued watching with growing apprehension, he dragged the fourth wall over and attached that section not with nails, but with a set of large brass hinges.

Now the structure looked like a tall, narrow, upright box with a door. Instead of a lock, which Tanner suspected would have taken too long to install, he simply took a short, very thick piece of wood from the tool kit and screwed it into the equally thick edge of one wall. When he twisted the chunk of wood sideways, it barred the door from opening every bit as effectively as a lock.

The cuckoo clock struck the hour of eight. Tanner was astonished. She had been watching him work for two hours? Two *hours*?

And Silly hadn't arrived. Tanner was sure no one had come up the walk. There would have been movement on the screen. She would have noticed it.

So he hadn't been lying. Something *had* happened to Silly. An accident? What, she'd burned her arm on the oven? Slipped on a freshly mopped floor and thrown her back out? Cut her hand on a glass that broke when she was drying it?

It had to be something like that. Couldn't be anything worse.

But how did *he* know about the accident, whatever it was? Had he been watching the house, like one of those stalkers that seemed to be constantly on the news lately? And seen Silly hurrying off to a doctor with her burned elbow or bleeding hand or bad back? Was that how he knew?

Tanner's hands felt clammy. "Tell me what that box is for," she demanded. Only eight A.M. What time would Charlie come?

She didn't want him showing up while this crazy carpenter was still holding that vicious-looking claw hammer in his hand.

"This is for you," he said. He walked around in front of the box and the worm-like lips of his mask slipped upward. "Nice work, don't you think? Considering the time constraints and all."

"For me?" Tanner, her face almost as gray as his mask, shrank further back into the couch. "It's for me?"

"Absolutely." He pushed the chunk of wood straight up and pulled open the crude "door," letting Tanner catch a glimpse of the interior. Small, so small. Not very wide, not very deep, only a few inches taller than he was. And dark. Small and dark.

Just like a coffin.

He swung the door shut and pushed the wooden bar down across it. "This is your Time Out booth," he said cheerfully.

"Time out?" Tanner stared at him. "What are you talking about?"

"Time out, time out," he said impatiently, waving one hand at her, "haven't you ever heard of time out? Weren't you ever disciplined as a kid? Didn't you have to go sit in a corner? Weren't you ever sent to your room to think about your misdeeds?"

Her mother hadn't been much of a disciplinarian. No cookies for a week, that was about as tough as her mother got.

"Well," he continued, this time more patiently, "this is where you're going to go when you do something wrong."

"Something wrong?"

"Is there an echo in here?" he shouted angrily. His voice sounded, then, vaguely familiar. "Quit questioning everything I say! Why don't you just *listen*? When people don't do as they're told, they have to have time out."

Tanner's jaw dropped.

"If you do what I say, if you're good as gold," he continued, "you won't have to go in there. But if you give me any trouble at all," he spread his hands helplessly, "well, I'll have no choice."

He gave the door of the box a gentle kick. "I'll have to see to it that you're properly disciplined. So!" he cried cheerfully, "we're all set!" And dropping the hammer back into the open toolbox, he plopped into the leather chair.

Although she couldn't see it, Tanner was convinced that a huge smile of satisfaction lit the face under the mask.

She sat up very straight on the couch. "I'm not going into that thing," she said with false bravado. "I don't care what you do to me, I'm not going in there. And you can't make me."

She was sorry the minute the words left her mouth, but it was too late.

In one eye-blinking instant, he was out of the chair and in front of her and grasping her sweatshirt with one fist while the other fist yanked on her hair. She cried out in pain, but he was already dragging her over to the box. Yanking the door open. Pushing her inside, face first.

The door slammed, taking the little bit of light with it, and Tanner heard the heavy chunk of wood being angrily flipped into place.

She was inside the tall, narrow coffin.

And she was locked in.

Chapter 8

At the Sigma Chi house, Charlie Cochran's roommate, Mark, awakened to find Charlie sitting on the edge of his unmade bed, holding a piece of paper in his hands.

"Geez, Charlie, you look like hell!" Mark said, dragging himself upright. "Whatsamatter, somebody die?"

Charlie didn't answer. He'd been awake all night, not even attempting to lie down and close his eyes. He'd alternated throughout the night between pacing the room or sitting on his bed or standing at the wide window overlooking a darkened campus brightened only by the walkway lamp posts and a few random lights still on in other houses along fraternity row. And he had read and reread the note signed with Tanner's name, struggling to understand what it meant, as if he were trying to decipher a message written in code.

Mark rubbed his eyes. "What's wrong, Charlie?" He was awake now, and the sight of his normally easygoing roommate, hair askew, clothes rumpled, unsettled Mark. The planet had to be off its axis if Charlie Cochran hadn't slept like a baby. "Something happen to Tanner?"

Charlie looked over at Mark as if realizing for the first time that he wasn't alone in the room. "I don't know," he said slowly, thoughtfully. Then he got up, scooped his jacket off the bed, and left the room.

Shrugging, Mark lay back down, deciding that if Charlie wasn't willing to share his troubles, Charlie's roommate might as well catch another forty winks. Wednesday . . . first class at nine . . . no rush . . . early yet . . .

Mark was asleep again in less than a minute.

Charlie, feeling as if he had just endured the longest night of his life, went first to Lester. Hurrying across the chilly, gray campus, empty of all but a few hardy early-risers, he thought about Tanner's note.

I can't stay in this house alone. Tanner had written that?

It was her handwriting. He knew it well. They were constantly writing each other little notes, full of silly things: remarks about a class or teacher, the latest joke, plans for the evening.

But *why* would Tanner write *those* words? She had never, not once, expressed any fear about having that house all to herself. Tanner wasn't afraid of being alone. As far as he could tell, she wasn't afraid of anything, not even her father, a cold fish if there ever was one. Charlie liked that about Tanner, that she wasn't afraid. Not an ounce of paranoia in her anywhere. He thought that probably came from practically raising herself.

So why would she suddenly decide she couldn't handle living alone, and take off to join her mother in parts unknown?

She wouldn't. She just wouldn't.

The note was crazy. It made no sense.

But he had gone to the house and rung that doorbell until he'd thought his finger would fall off. Had heard the bell pealing inside the house, loud and clear. No answer. Even after he'd finally noticed the note, suspended from the mailbox by a clothespin, flapping in the wind like a miniature bedsheet, he'd continued to jab at the bell.

But Tanner hadn't come running, that great smile on her face, apologizing for taking so long to answer because she'd been in the shower and hadn't heard the bell.

Even if, for some bizarre reason, Tanner had decided she really didn't want to stay in the house alone that first night, she would never have gone off to join her mother. Tanner loved Salem, loved being at college. She wasn't wild about living with Dr. Chill, but she loved school and campus and everything that went with it. So she wouldn't have left. She would have moved in with Jodie and Sandy, or tried to get a dorm room of her own.

And she would never, *never* have gone anywhere without calling him first. No way.

The whole thing was nuts.

Jodie and Sandy hadn't heard from Tanner.

Charlie's rugged, handsome face fell when Sandy shook her head and said, "Haven't heard a word, Charlie." She asked to see the note, held so tightly and for so long in Charlie's left hand, the edges were crumpled like used tissue paper. Sandy read it and then silently handed it to Jodie.

"She wouldn't do this," Jodie announced flatly when her eyes had zoomed over the words. "She wouldn't! It's a joke, that's all. Where did you find this?"

He told them.

"Well, someone else put it there," Jodie declared. "Tanner didn't."

"It's her handwriting," Charlie said wearily, hating to admit it.

"Maybe she got scared, being alone," Sandy offered. "That's a big house, and the housekeeper doesn't sleep over."

"The housekeeper!" Charlie cried, striding over to the telephone nestled on a bedside table amid papers and books and framed photographs. "The housekeeper will know if Tanner got home okay yesterday. And if she wasn't willing to spend the night there alone." About to pick up the receiver, he stopped, a blank look on his face. "Only I don't know her name. Tanner always calls her 'Silly.' You guys know what her real name is?"

They shook their heads. "But someone at the administration building probably would," Jodie said. "If you called and said you needed to know the name of Dr. Leo's housekeeper, they'd probably tell you. I think the faculty's domestic staff is hired through Butler Hall, just like the maintenance staff is."

Charlie quickly dialed the main office at Butler Hall, but there was no answer.

"Too early," Jodie pointed out. "Listen, Charlie, why don't you go back to the Sigma Chi house and sleep for an hour or so? You look terrible, and we can't really do anything until you get that telephone number. You didn't sleep at all last night, did you?"

He didn't answer. But the faint shadows under his eyes and the beard stubble on his face answered for him. Still, he stubbornly shook his head no. "How can I sleep?" he asked miserably.

Jodie nodded. "Well, then, let's go downstairs and get you some coffee, okay? And maybe an egg or two wouldn't hurt. Then we'll call Butler Hall again. By that time, someone should be there."

Charlie didn't move away from the telephone.

"Come on, Charlie," Jodie persisted, pushing her glasses back up on her nose, something she did constantly when she was frustrated, "you know what Vince always says. When in doubt, eat. He's right. It always works for me. And if you won't eat anything, at least come have a cup of coffee. Our coffee here is guaranteed to keep you awake for at least the next twelve hours. That's a promise."

That worked, because Charlie knew he was going to need something to keep him awake. He wouldn't sleep again, he vowed silently, until he had answers to all of his questions.

"Okay, I'll go," he said, "but you'd better be right about the coffee."

Vince and Philip were already seated at a rear table in the small cafeteria in Lester's basement. Although Philip reacted to Tanner's note with the same disbelief that Jodie had, Vince wasn't as certain that Tanner hadn't written it.

"She didn't like living with old Stiffneck," he said, stirring his coffee with a pencil. "She never kept that a secret. So maybe she figured this was a good time to pack up and leave, since he wasn't there to throw a fit and try to stop her."

"In the first place," Jodie said, "I don't think he *would* have tried to stop her. He would have stood in the doorway with that supercilious look on his face and said something like, 'Well, if this is your choice, Tanner, you're an adult and I can't stop you from making it.' He'd do that before he'd ever admit that he actually wanted her to stay. And in the second place, Tanner wouldn't have gone anywhere without calling one of us first, agreed?"

The doubtful expression on Vince's long, narrow face remained. "She might not have had time to call. Or maybe she tried and your line was busy."

"You're missing the point," Charlie said quietly. "I don't think for a minute that she was trying to call any of us, because I don't think for a minute that she was leaving. Not the house, not campus, not us. She wouldn't, that's all. She just wouldn't." He sipped hot coffee for a minute, then put the mug down and added, "We're just spinning our wheels here. I don't know what's going on, but I don't like it." He glanced down at his wristwatch. "I'm calling Butler Hall. I need that housekeeper's name and address."

Vince glanced up from his scrambled eggs. "You mean Tanner's housekeeper?"

Charlie nodded.

"Oh, it's Sills. Mavis Sills. She lives in that new apartment complex right along the riverbank in Twin Falls. I think it's River Street."

Charlie looked startled. "How do you know all that? I didn't know it."

"A friend of Sills, Sunshine Mooney, is the housemother at Lindy's sorority house." Lindy was Vince's current girlfriend. "Lindy says Sunshine talks about her friend Silly a lot: where they're going on vacation together, how when Sunshine retires she's going to move into Silly's apartment complex, that kind of stuff. I picked up on the name 'Silly', thought it was funny, and that's when Lindy told me it was Tanner's housekeeper and her real name was Mavis Sills." Vince grinned. "Now there's a pair of names for you, Sunshine and Silly.

Sounds like a comedy act, doesn't it?"

"There!" Sandy told Charlie emphatically, "now you don't have to waste time calling Butler Hall. You can call the housekeeper and find out why Tanner left."

"She *didn't* leave!" Charlie, dark eyes blazing, fairly bit off the words. "How many times do I have to say it?"

Chagrined, Sandy mumbled, "Sorry. I meant, you can ask her where Tanner is."

But there was no answer at the housekeeper's apartment. Charlie let the phone ring a dozen times, refusing to give up until Jodie urged gently, "Charlie, give it up, she's not *there*. Come on! We'll try something else."

They were all clustered around one of the pay phones in Lester's lobby. "Why don't we just hike on over to Tanner's?" Philip suggested. "Maybe the housekeeper is already there. That could be why she isn't answering at her place, Charlie."

Charlie quickly dialed the Leo home. "If Silly is there, why isn't she answering?" he asked a moment later when, again, there was no response to the insistent ringing.

"She could still be on her way," Sandy said.

Giving up, Charlie hung up the phone.

"Let's go over there," Jodie said eagerly. "Silly will be there by then, and Tanner could be there, too. Maybe she stayed with someone else last night, although you'd think she'd call her best friends first, wouldn't you? But let's face it, Tanner has lots of friends to choose from."

"Well, let's just go find out," Charlie said, and led the way out of the building.

But, though they rang the front doorbell at Tanner's house, then went around to the back and pounded on the back door, and then circled the house on the outside, going from room to room and rapping on the outside of every window they could reach, the big brick house showed no signs of life.

It was as still, as silent, as death.

Chapter 9

Tanner, imprisoned in the tall, dark narrow box, was completely unaware that morning of Charlie's arrival. She couldn't see the surveillance screens, couldn't hear the insistent doorbell or the pounding on wood or rapping on glass. Her friends came and went without her knowledge.

Tanner was aware only of the narrow confines of her tiny cell. Because the hastily constructed booth was not soundproof like the music room, she *did* hear her captor leave, heard him close and lock the door.

Before she'd been angry, upset, and yes, afraid. Now she was desperate. There was barely enough room in the box to lift her arms from her sides, let alone turn around and face front. Even if she did manage to turn around, the door was barred against her. Hadn't she heard, very clearly, the thick chunk of wood being twisted into place? There was no mistaking that sound. She was locked into this terrible place, like an animal in a cage. Worse. Cages had bars, and you could see out.

Although there was air inside what Tanner had come to think of as "the coffin," she knew it would quickly grow stale. It was already stuffy. Beads of sweat began to gather on her forehead, clinging to her hair. The smell of fresh-cut lumber was giving her a headache.

It was dark, but there were tiny pinpricks of light slipping in between narrow gaps in the boards. There were more, larger gaps at the corners, where the walls had been joined.

Tanner tried to peer through one of the small cracks, but could see only an edge of the fireplace mantel, which did her no good at all.

She managed to turn around, facing the front of her narrow cell. She pushed against the door. Then pushed again, harder this time. Her breath came in shallow gasps. She wished that she were wearing heavy work boots so she could kick at the door. Bare feet were useless.

She reached out to press against the walls on either side of her, as if by doing so, she could push them farther away, giving her more room. She was suddenly desperate for more room. The lack of space made her feel as if she were being squeezed like an accordion.

It was hopeless. She wasn't going to get out of here on her own. Hastily put together or not, the tall, narrow box made an effective prison.

What was he *doing* to her? And why was he doing it?

Her palms still pressing against the side walls, her back against the rear wall, Tanner sank slowly to the floor, where she had to bend her knees for lack of room.

She placed her hands in her lap and let her chin rest on her chest. Maybe none of this was really happening. It couldn't be real. How could it?

She stared into the darkness, her eyes widening with hope. Maybe it *wasn't* real. She couldn't be sure exactly when, but at some point after she'd arrived home, maybe she'd fallen asleep. Maybe . . . maybe when she went upstairs to look for Silly.

Yes . . . yes! That had to be it. Of course! She remembered standing in the middle of her bedroom when she hadn't been able to find Silly. That must have been when she'd gone over to lie down on her bed, probably intending to just rest for a minute. And she'd fallen sound asleep instead.

Which made everything after that a dream. A horrible, creepy nightmare but still, not *real*!

So she wasn't actually sitting in this narrow, airless box. She was lying on her bed upstairs, sound asleep. Silly was somewhere in the house or the backyard and there was no intruder who looked like something risen from the grave.

Feeling much better, Tanner leaned against the back wall of the coffin and closed her eyes, deciding that the best thing to do was wait patiently for the dream to be over. Not that she had a choice.

She didn't hear the music room door open. Her first awareness that she was no longer alone came when a sudden burst of light told her the door to the coffin had been yanked open.

Shielding her eyes against the light, Tanner raised her head.

The repulsive gray mask stared down at her. "Well, how do you like it? Not much fun, is it? But then, it's not supposed to be. It's actually been proven very effective in disciplining those wild, unruly creatures whom society chooses to call 'difficult' or 'wayward.' Wayward youth, ah, what an expression. Implies that they're going in the wrong direction, right?" He laughed bitterly. "Like the people in charge actually know what the *right* direction is! That hasn't been *my* experience, I can tell you."

Tanner blinked. It hadn't been a dream,

after all? Disappointment washed over her, painful as an acid bath.

"Yes, ma'am," he continued, one hand holding the door open, "this is what we call 'The Booth.' Looks kind of like a coffin, doesn't it? This is where people are sent when they break a rule, no matter how slight the infraction. Maybe they mouth off, or resort to a sharp kick or a punch to settle a dispute, or maybe they don't make their bed one morning because they're in a hurry, or they don't hang up their clothes exactly the right way. So they have to go into The Booth."

"What are you *talking* about?" Tanner cried, struggling awkwardly to her feet. Her legs were cramped, and she had to stamp her bare feet on the wooden floor to restore circulation.

"Never mind. That's in the past. For me, anyway. Look, you said you were hungry," he said flatly. "You can come out and eat. But if you give me any trouble at all, you'll be back in The Booth so fast, your head will spin. And you'll stay there until your hair turns gray. Come on out of there."

Tanner, her legs stiff, stepped out.

"You're lucky you're alone in the house," he said. "If there were lots of people here, they'd all hammer on The Booth when they walked by, and kick at it and yell things, so you'd never be able to sleep, even though that's what you want to do more than anything, to make the time go faster."

Tanner was wallowing in the bitter truth that none of this was a dream. No nightmare, after all. She hadn't fallen asleep on her bed upstairs. It had all happened, every last horrible second of it. And it was still happening. "It was bad enough without any noise," she said. She was so glad to be out of that horrible box, she almost felt grateful to him. She had to remind herself that he was the one who had put her in there in the first place.

Her teeth felt gritty, her hair was a mass of tangles, and she yearned desperately for a shower and clean clothes. Maybe, if she did everything he told her to, she could talk him into letting her go upstairs alone for half an hour.

How long was he planning on holding her here? Where was Silly? And why hadn't Charlie come back, looking for her?

"You can call me Sigmund," her jailer said abruptly, as if she'd asked his name. "Just Sigmund."

"Sigmund?" When she was very young, her mother had called her father that when she was mad at him. Her voice had been sharp and sarcastic. "As in Freud?" Tanner asked just as sharply.

"As in Sigmund." He took her elbow, gripping it firmly, and led her out of the music room and down the hall to the empty kitchen.

I don't want to call him anything, Tanner thought, glancing quickly around the kitchen for some sign of Silly, and finding none. I don't want him here long enough to have to give him a name.

If she could only get a grip on what was happening. But it was all so unbelievable, so Twilight-Zonish. She was trapped inside some crazy video game, except that someone else had the controls.

"You now have four minutes," he said. "Why don't you have a nice bowl of ice cream?"

Out of the music room for the first time, Tanner was much more interested in escape than in food, although her stomach was pleading otherwise. This could be her only chance to get away.

If she went with him to the freezer for ice cream, if she maneuvered her position on the porch cleverly enough, she just might be able to race out the back door and scream for help before he could grab her.

It was worth a try. She *had* to get away

from him. Out of this house and away from him.

"Ice cream sounds good," she agreed, and went to the cupboard to get a bowl, then to the silverware drawer for a spoon and a metal scoop.

"I want some, too," he said, sounding offended, and followed her steps to collect his own bowl and spoon. "It's your favorite, strawberry ripple."

Tanner paused halfway between the sink and the kitchen table. "How do you know?" she asked, conscious of a new uneasiness beginning to slide up her spine.

"What?"

"How do *you* know what kind of ice cream Silly bought?"

"Oh. I . . . I saw the note she left, and I checked to see what kind she got. Just curious, that's all."

Which would have made sense, except for one thing. Tanner had pocketed the note from Silly. She had come home, read the note, and put it in the pocket of her sweatpants. It was still there, slightly the worse for wear.

So, if he'd come into the house after Tanner got home, he couldn't possibly have seen Silly's note.

Then . . . how did he know that Silly had bought ice cream, and what flavor it was?

Had he already been *in* the house when Tanner arrived? Hiding? Waiting?

It was then that Tanner realized exactly what part of the note had bothered her, the thing that had been niggling at some small part of her brain ever since she'd read it. It was the signature. "Mavis." Silly had left notes before. She never signed them "Mavis." She always signed them "Silly," looping her letter l's broad and wide, like letters written in the sky by an airplane.

But *this* note had been signed "Mavis."

Because . . . Tanner's throat closed . . . because Silly hadn't written it.

He had.

No wonder the note hadn't sounded anything like Silly. That explained, too, why it had been printed instead of sprawled across the page in Silly's usual careless scrawl. He hadn't wanted to take a chance on trying to fake Silly's longhand.

Why would he write a note telling Tanner there was ice cream in the freezer?

Instead of moving on into the back porch off the kitchen, Tanner turned to face him. He was busy collecting a spoon from the wall of cupboards and drawers opposite her. "How did you know I like strawberry ripple ice cream?" she asked.

The gray mask swiveled toward her. "What?"

"How did you know?"

"Me? I didn't buy the ice cream. What are you, nuts? Your housekeeper bought it."

No, she didn't, Tanner thought with stunning clarity. She didn't write the note, so she didn't buy the ice cream, either. *You* did. But why?

The answer came from somewhere in the back of her mind, delivered with the same stunning force. He had bought the ice cream and written the note to get her out to the freezer on the back porch.

Why? If it hadn't been for the coffin, she'd have been terrified that he planned to force her into the low, squat freezer on the back porch. But if that was his plan, he never would have taken so much time and effort to build that horrible wooden box in the music room, would he?

Tanner's brain whirled. What was going *on*?

Why hadn't Silly left her own note about dinner before she'd left yesterday? She *always* left a note. Always.

If he'd been hiding in the house *before* Tanner got home, wouldn't he have run into Silly?

"Speaking of the housekeeper," she said, her voice nearly strangling with anxiety, "did you by any chance see her when you got here yesterday, whenever that was? I mean, she was supposed to show up for work today, and she's not here. I figure, if you saw her, you might know if she's sick or something."

"Well, if she's not here," he said brusquely, "I guess that means she *is* sick or something, right? Now, can we please cut out all this stupid chitchat and go get our ice cream?"

Tanner was starving. But a feeling far stronger than hunger kept her fingers clenched around the edge of the table. She couldn't have explained it to anyone, not even Charlie, but a sudden conviction that she should not, under any circumstances, go near that back porch, nailed her feet to the blue and white tile.

"I said come on," Sigmund said rudely, and gave her elbow a push.

Tanner knew she had no choice. Reluctantly, she let go of the table and forced her bare feet, cold against the tile, to shuffle along beside him.

She was only a few feet from the doorway leading to the porch when she saw it. A scrap of vivid rust and bright yellow material hanging over the edge of the freezer, underneath the closed lid.

She knew that material well. It was part of an outfit that Silly was very proud of, because she'd made it herself — a short-sleeved cotton dress with a triangular headscarf and an apron that tied at the waist.

Tanner tried to tell herself that the apron or the headscarf must have fallen off when Silly was putting something in or taking something out of the freezer. She tried so hard to believe that.

But she knew it wasn't true.

Tanner held back, her bare toes gripping the cold tile.

He pushed, urging her onward.

"No," she said quietly. Her eyes, filled with apprehension, stared at the telltale bit of bright yellow and rust fabric trailing, oh, so innocently, from underneath the freezer lid.

Her breath caught in her throat.

Silly wasn't at her apartment, hadn't been at the dentist's.

Silly hadn't left early, *wouldn't* have left early last night when they had planned to celebrate with homemade chocolate cake. It was still sitting, half-eaten, on the kitchen table.

And Silly hadn't shown up for work today.

Silly was nowhere to be seen, and her apron or headscarf was sticking out of the freezer. Tanner couldn't bear to look at it for another second. Her chest ached from the sight of the rust and yellow fabric.

But when she turned her head away, a rough

hand came from behind and buffeted her head sideways so that her eyes were once again facing the freezer.

"Go ahead!" Sigmund ordered, his hand pushing against the small of Tanner's back.

Tanner felt sick. "You didn't hurt her, did you? You didn't hurt Silly?"

The hand pushed again. "Your housekeeper's name is Silly? Well, that's pretty stupid." A low, wicked snicker accompanied a push that sent Tanner up against the front of the freezer. "Or should I say that's pretty *silly*?" Another snicker. "Open the freezer, Tanner!"

Dizzy, Tanner leaned forward, onto the freezer, which came up to her waist. Her right hand brushed against the scrap of apron protruding from the top.

"I *said* open it up!" he commanded, shoving at Tanner's right arm.

And even though she knew, without a doubt, that he had it in him to kill her, even though she knew that as surely as she knew her own name, she lifted her head, staring straight ahead at the knotty pine paneling behind the freezer and said clearly, defiantly, "No. No, I won't. I won't open it."

She had no idea why she said the words. If she had thought about it carefully, she probably wouldn't have defied someone she was now convinced could take her life without batting an eyelash. "Okay, okay, I'll open it," she would have said if she'd been thinking clearly.

But she wasn't thinking at all. Her mind was too stunned, as if she'd just received a second sharp blow to the skull. The shock of seeing that scrap of fabric hanging from the freezer, when Silly was nowhere to be seen, had rendered her brain useless. Everything she did now was purely instinctive, and every instinct she possessed screamed at her not to open the freezer lid.

There was a cold, angry silence behind her.

Tanner's breath came in short, panicky gasps.

The angry silence lasted for a thousand years.

Then it was broken by Sigmund's husky voice saying, "Okay, then, I'll open it!"

Something inside Tanner screamed, NO! She stiffened her spine and slammed both hands, palms down, upon the top of the lid in an effort to keep it closed.

In vain. The arms that reached out from behind her and began to pull up on the lid were much stronger than hers.

She pressed downward with every ounce of strength she had left.

Laughing, he pulled upward.

In spite of her efforts, the lid lifted slightly. Not much, just an inch or two. Tanner was proud of her strength as she battled against his obvious superiority. Only an inch or two.

But an inch or two was enough.

She wasn't going to look down, into the freezer, wasn't, *wasn't*. She was going to keep her eyes focused on the knotty pine walls behind the freezer. She would concentrate on studying the different sizes and shapes of the darker circles of wood. She was *not*, ever, going to look down.

But he took one hand off the freezer lid, grabbed a fistful of her hair, and pushed her head down, forcing her to look.

She saw almost nothing. Almost. First, more of the apron. The part of the apron that had been trapped inside the freezer had stiffened, as if heavily starched. Then she saw a pocket, with the corner of a tissue poking out over the edge. Silly had allergies, and never went anywhere without a pocketful of tissues.

Tanner struggled to avert her eyes, crying out in pain and fear, but the hand on her hair kept her head immobile and there was nowhere else for her eyes to look but inside the freezer. The lid lifted a tiny bit more.

Bangles . . . cheap, silver bangles, on a thick,

freckled wrist. The wrist that had handed out cookies and cold drinks and hot cups of tea and sandwiches cut in the shape of hearts, that had made the bed in the apricot and white bedroom, had ironed blouses and dresses, washed jeans and sweatshirts, had pulled a clean tissue from an apron pocket and handed it to Tanner to wipe her eyes when she was homesick for Ashtabula.

That wrist was once a healthy, freckled pink. But the bangled wrist that Tanner looked down upon now was stiff and bluish-gray, like a frozen dove she'd found in the backyard in Ohio one winter.

Tanner saw no more than that. That one small glimpse was enough to make her gasp. Her head snapped backward against the fist grasping her hair and, without a sound, she reeled off into a black void.

Her body folded into itself as if someone had removed all of her bones.

Chapter 10

Only Jodie was willing to go with Charlie to the campus police. The others felt that while it was weird that Tanner had taken off without letting any of them know, the note *was* in her handwriting.

"The police will take one look at that note," Philip said as they finally gave up their hammering and pounding and bell-ringing at the Leo house and left, "and they'll decide you've got no case at all. Tanner's eighteen, Charlie. She's allowed to go wherever she wants. And she left a note saying where she was going. That's what they'll tell you."

"She didn't *want* to go join her mother!" Charlie said heatedly.

"Yeah, but try telling the cops that, when that's what it says in the note. The note that Tanner *signed*."

Sandy and Vince, like Philip, saw no point

in going to the police. "They'll just think she didn't want to stay in the house alone," Sandy said, "like the note says." Vince nodded, adding, "That note's your problem, Charlie. Without it, you might have a case. I mean, since Tanner isn't where she's supposed to be. But . . ."

"Then I won't show them the note," Charlie said firmly, folding the note and stashing it in a back pocket of his jeans.

Sandy was visibly shocked. "Charlie! You can't do that! Tanner *wrote* that note. That's hiding evidence."

"It's only evidence if there's been some kind of crime," Charlie pointed out. "And that's what I'm trying to find out . . . if something criminal has happened to Tanner. If the note's going to keep me from doing that, then I'm hiding it."

"Charlie!" Jodie said quietly, eyes behind her glasses wide with alarm. "You don't really think something criminal has happened to Tanner, do you?"

"I don't want to. But this just isn't like Tanner, not at all. The thing is, you guys are right, if I show the cops the note, they won't help us find out anything. *We* know Tanner wouldn't have taken off without telling us." Charlie hesitated. "We *do* know that, right?"

"Right!" Jodie said emphatically. Vince, Sandy, and Philip only nodded halfheartedly.

They had turned off Faculty Row and were standing in front of the science building, a tall, light-colored brick structure. Students and teachers hurried to and from the building through a light, chilly drizzle. Sloane Currier drove by in his bright red sportscar, rolling down the window as he reached them. "What's up, guys?"

Charlie quickly filled him in.

"If you ask me," Sloane said, wiping at the mist coating the inside of his windshield with the sleeve of his expensive red sweater, "Doc Leo probably had second thoughts about leaving a college kid alone in that house of his and called to order Tanner to Hawaii, on the double."

"Then why," Charlie asked, "would she say in the note that she was going to see her mother?"

"Because," Sloane said calmly, "she knows we can't stand her father's guts and wouldn't want us to think she'd cave in to him, right? So she lied."

"That's stupid," Jodie cried. "Tanner wouldn't lie about something like that. *You* might," she added scornfully, "but Tanner wouldn't."

Sloane's smile thinned. "No need to be snide, Joellen. Anyway, Vince and Sandy are right. Going to the law is a waste of time. Especially with that note that Tanner wrote herself. They'll think you all need a couple of hours on the couch with the fink-shrink, Dr. Leo."

They all knew that one of the reasons Sloane detested the psychology teacher was Dr. Leo had once reported him for cheating. Only the fact that Sloane's father, a Salem alumnus, contributed generously to the college, had kept him in school. But he'd been on probation and that had not made Sloane happy.

"I'm not taking the note to the cops," Charlie said, his mouth grim. "It'll only get in the way. Without it, the police might be willing to check things out."

But they weren't. Even without the note, which Charlie kept safely tucked away in his jeans pocket, campus security declined to take any action.

"Can't do a thing for seventy-two hours," the officer told Charlie and Jodie. Tanner's other friends had gone about their business, convinced that a visit to the police would be a total waste of time. They were right. "She's not a little kid," the pair was told. "If there was some sign of forced entry, something suspicious, we could investigate. But you said the house looked okay, right?"

Charlie nodded reluctantly, wishing he'd had the foresight to break a cellar window at the Leo house.

"Your friend probably just didn't want to stay in the house alone now that Dr. Leo's out of town."

"Tanner's not like that," Charlie argued, but he could see that it was hopeless.

"You should have showed him the note," Jodie said when they were standing outside on the quad. The drizzle had thickened into a steady rain shower. Her hair was already wet, strands of it plastered against her cheeks as if they'd been glued there. "Maybe he'd have some way of telling whether or not Tanner actually wrote it."

"Oh, she wrote it, all right," Charlie said darkly, hunching his shoulders against the rain. "The question is, *why* did she write it? Why *would* she? He couldn't tell us that, could he?"

"No," Jodie admitted, "I guess he couldn't."

They had classes to go to. Although Jodie felt that falling behind in her own schedule wouldn't do Tanner any good, Charlie knew he'd never be able to concentrate and had already decided to cut. Disheartened, they separated, promising to call each other later and decide what to do next.

Charlie Cochran, like Tanner, wasn't used to feeling afraid. But he felt afraid now. It was a new sensation. The blood in his veins felt cold and he could feel the rhythm of his heart and his pulse speeding up, pounding erratically. The ground underneath his feet, slick with rain, felt unsafe, as if he were walking up a muddy slope instead of on level cement.

Tanner *had* to be in that house. She wouldn't have gone off anywhere without calling him first. And if she *was* in the house, and she hadn't answered the doorbell, there had to be a reason. Maybe she'd fallen asleep in the music room. She wouldn't have heard the doorbell in there, wouldn't have heard them pounding on the doors, rapping on the windows.

The only problem with that theory was, Tanner hated that room. Why would she go in there and spend the night?

Maybe just to prove that she could? That would be like Tanner.

There was only one way to find out for sure.

Charlie stuck his hands in the pockets of his bomber jacket, and shoulders hunched against the rain, struck out in the direction of Faculty Row.

He was about to kill two birds with one

stone. He would break into the Leo house and see for himself if Tanner had fallen asleep in the soundproof room. If she had, if she was safe and sound, that was one thing. But if she wasn't, this time when he went to the police, he could honestly report a broken window in the back door, because he was about to break that window himself. *Then* they'd come running, wouldn't they?

Two birds with one stone. It would help, one way or the other.

But what would really make him happy and melt the ice in his veins would be finding Tanner curled up on a couch in the music room, sound asleep.

Faculty Row was deserted. It was after ten o'clock, and most professors had morning classes. The street was quiet but for a dog or two barking, annoyed at being left out in the rain, the muted roar of a distant motorcycle, and the steady tap-tap-tap of the rain hitting new leaves on the trees overhead and slapping onto the sidewalk.

Tanner, Charlie thought intently as he hurried up the street, *be* there. Be asleep. Be okay. Please, Tanner.

He was so lost in his intense prayer to Tanner that he never heard the motorcycle approaching, didn't notice that the distant, muted sound had become louder. Charlie didn't even turn his head until its raucous roar grew so close, the heavy machine seemed to be on the sidewalk right behind him instead of on the road where it belonged.

Too late, Charlie realized with a lurch of his heart that *on the sidewalk* was exactly where the motorcycle was. It was bearing down upon him at top speed, its engine roaring so loudly, Charlie thought his eardrums would burst.

And too late, he shouted and threw himself sideways, his tall, wiry body toppling like an axed tree into the thick bushes fronting the Leos' picket fence.

With a loud, angry roar, the machine raced straight at Charlie, catching him in midflight. The bike sideswiped the fence and Charlie at the same time, splintering half a dozen pickets, and snapping the bone in Charlie's right arm like a twig.

A semiconscious Charlie landed with a sickening thud on the Leos' front lawn, his arm flopping uselessly.

The motorcycle roared away.

Chapter 11

The minute Tanner came to, she knew exactly where she was by the utter and complete silence. Back in the music room. She was lying on the couch, and she was alone. She knew this even before she groggily lifted her head to glance around. She sensed it.

She was right. There was no one else in the room. *He* was gone again.

Tanner sank back against the pillow, releasing a grateful sigh. He was gone. She was safe for now.

Immediately following that thought came another: what was she doing lying on the couch? The last thing she remembered was standing in the kitchen, her feet cold on the tile, her hand gripping the edge of the kitchen table. When had she moved from there back to the music room?

She thought the music room door was locked

again, but just to make sure, Tanner got up slowly and walked over to test the doorknob. It didn't budge when she tried to turn it. No big surprise.

How long had she been back in this room? What time had he taken her to the kitchen? Around nine?

Her eyes went to the cuckoo clock over the fireplace. Ten-thirty! Had she been asleep that long? Or had they been in the kitchen longer than she'd thought? Why couldn't she remember? What was wrong with her? Her brain felt as if it were wrapped in soft, thick, black velvet. Had he hit her over the head again?

She stood with her back to the door, shaking her head gently, glancing around the room again. The red tool kit was gone. She had hoped he would forget and leave it. There might have been something in there she could use to jimmy the door open. Of course, he'd never be that careless. Too much to hope for.

She was turning away from the door when she noticed movement on the screen of the surveillance camera sweeping the front yard. Looking more intently, she saw a scene of chaos outside.

An ambulance, its doors open, was backed up to the curb. A police car, its blue light whirling on the roof, was parked beside the emergency vehicle. A crowd of people edged the picket fence. A section of it was missing, Tanner noticed as, keeping her eyes on the screen, she backed up until her legs bumped into the couch. Automatically taking a seat, she kept watching the scene unfolding on the tiny screen.

Someone had been hurt. That was clear. An accident . . . had someone been hit by a car on Faculty Row? Hard to believe. Everyone drove very slowly up and down the street, aware that there might be children playing in the area.

But something *had* happened. Something bad.

Tanner jumped to her feet. What was *wrong* with her? Why was she still sitting here, doing nothing? It was awful that an accident had happened, but she would be insane not to take advantage of it. There were *people* out there, a whole crowd of them, people who could help her, could save her, if she could somehow get their attention. They were busy, rushing around, pulling a stretcher from the ambulance, but there had to be some way to signal them that she was imprisoned inside this house.

She might not get another chance like this.

Tanner surveyed the room frantically. There had to be a way to let them know she was in here. In any other room in the house, where the windows were placed at a normal height in the walls, she would simply have run to the glass and pounded until someone heard or saw her. But here, that wouldn't work.

And if it were night, she could have switched a lamp on and off repeatedly until someone noticed. Even with the windows so high up, the constant flickering of light would have been discernible. But while the skylight revealed a gray, gloomy day, it still wasn't dark enough outside for anyone to notice a lamp going on and off inside the house.

Tanner shook her head. The dim light from small table lamps wouldn't be reflected in those windows, anyway. They were too high up on the wall.

But . . . the lamps were small enough to *throw*.

Yanking the cord out of its socket, Tanner grabbed the small but heavy brass lamp from one end table and heaved it at one of two front windows up near the ceiling. Her aim was accurate. But the lamp slammed into the window without breaking the glass, bounced off, and fell back to the floor. When it hit the carpet, the white shade crumpled and the bulb exploded, embedding small fragments of fine, thin glass in the turquoise carpet.

Now I won't be able to walk over there by that wall, Tanner thought dispiritedly, since I don't have any shoes.

Of course her father had installed shatter-proof glass. Couldn't be too careful these days, Tanner thought bitterly. You just never knew when a band of ruffians might begin roaming the streets, tossing rocks at Doctor Leo's music room windows.

There was a heavy crystal candy dish on her father's desk. Tanner hoisted it, testing its weight, and since it felt hefty enough, she threw that, too.

With the same results. Although there was a sharp, cracking sound upon impact, the window remained intact. The dish bounced away harmlessly, landing on the grand piano with a second sharp crack. This impact split the candy dish into four even chunks, as if it had been sectioned like a piece of fruit. The four pieces tumbled from the piano to the floor, joining the light bulb fragments imbedded in the carpet.

All I'm doing, Tanner thought numbly, is tossing glass into the carpet, as if I were planting seeds.

Dispirited, her eyes returned to the screen above her.

Any other time, someone passing by might have noticed a lamp and a candy dish striking the window from inside, in spite of the height of the windows facing front. But the scene outside was so chaotic, Tanner realized, that it would take far more than a mere table lamp or a candy dish to catch anyone's attention just now.

What *was* going on out there? She'd been so preoccupied with her own need to catch someone's attention, she hadn't tried to figure out what had happened. Obviously, an accident. What kind?

She moved closer to the camera. The picture wasn't very good to begin with, and the rain didn't help. It was like looking at a miniature picture through gauze. Still, she studied the screen carefully.

Suddenly she realized it wasn't just a crowd of strangers outside.

Wasn't that Jodie, in a yellow raincoat, standing there, her hands over her mouth? And there was Vince, and behind him, Sandy, Philip, and Sloane.

Where was Charlie? Why wasn't he with them?

Seeing her friends so close and yet so unreachable drove Tanner wild. She began jumping up and down, waving her arms and screaming, "I'm here, you guys, I'm right here, in the house! Come and get me, please, please, come and get me!"

Unaware, they continued to stand in a small group in the rain, next to the ambulance, staring down at something on the ground out of camera range.

Tanner stopped jumping and fell silent. They were all there, Philip and Jodie, Sandy and Vince and Sloane. Why wasn't Charlie? Something bad had happened, and they had all heard about it and come running. Why hadn't Charlie come running with them?

Where was he?

She watched, her mouth slightly open, her hands clenched together, as Sandy looked up at Philip and said something. Philip shook his head, and then a policeman came along and ordered them out of the way. It was like watching a silent movie . . . the figures moved and mouthed things and Tanner couldn't hear anything they said, but she could tell what was going on.

Peering more closely, she realized that Sandy and Jodie were crying.

Jodie never cried. Not at sad movies, not over a bad grade, not when she was homesick, never.

Why was Jodie crying now?

A shoe . . . Tanner saw a shoe, in the lower lefthand corner of the screen. A sneaker, wet and muddy and very large.

And suddenly, she wanted to scream.

It wasn't as if she could say she recognized the shoe. Not that shoe particularly. There had to be hundreds of sneakers exactly like that one, right down to the size, on the campus of Salem University.

But the fact that made her want to scream was, four of her friends were standing out in the street in front of her house looking at something that upset them very much. And the fifth person, who should have been standing right there with them, wasn't. The fifth person, someone she loved a lot, someone who had very large feet, and wore very large sneakers, just like the ones lying on the ground on the screen, was not out there watching as the ambulance attendants rushed forward with a stretcher.

Was Charlie not watching with the others because Charlie was the person lying on the ground needing a stretcher?

Something bad had happened to Charlie?

Then she saw the figure being lifted onto the stretcher, one bloody arm in the leather bomber jacket extended, and knew for an absolute fact that something terrible *had* happened to Charlie Cochran in her front yard.

And then she screamed.

Although she screamed and screamed, and shouted Charlie's name through her tears, and ran in a frenzy to the front wall to pound on it with both fists, not even noticing that along the way she had stepped on glass and sliced open the soles of both feet, although she pounded and screamed and shouted until her hands were swollen and her voice was hoarse, no one outside the house heard her.

When, exhausted, she returned to the middle of the room, her lacerated feet weaving a pattern of narrow and wide stripes of thick, wet scarlet across the turquoise carpet, and she looked up at the camera with red, swollen eyes, there was nothing on the screen but a gray sheet of rain.

The ambulance had gone, its shrill siren unheard in the music room.

The police car was gone.

Her friends were gone.

Charlie-on-the-stretcher was gone.

No one had heard her.

Crying out softly, Tanner sank to the floor,

Chapter 12

Because Charlie's injuries weren't life-threatening, he was taken to the campus infirmary instead of the Medical Center in Twin Falls. His friends were relieved to learn from the doctor on duty that other than a clean, simple fracture of his arm and some cuts and bruises, Charlie was in good shape. And yes, they could see him. But he would be kept in the infirmary until the following day and watched for any sign of concussion or other injuries.

When his friends were encircling Charlie's bed, Jodie commented gently, "Your face is the same color as your pillowcase. You must have been scared to death. I don't blame you." Then, more soberly, she added, "What happened, Charlie? Why did you go back to Tanner's? And why were you walking in the road instead of on the sidewalk? Did you see the car that hit you?"

Charlie was groggy from the medication, but fighting sleep. There was something he needed to tell them. Everyone had been so busy getting him into the ambulance, rushing him off to the infirmary . . . what was it he needed to tell them? "But I *was* on the sidewalk," he murmured. "Motorcycle. . . ."

His head lolled to one side, he whispered, "Tanner," and then Charlie was asleep, eyes closed, mouth slightly open, his breathing deep and even.

"What did he say?" Jodie asked, turning to Sandy.

Sandy frowned. "I thought he said 'motorcycle.' "

"And he said he was on the sidewalk," Philip added. "He got hit by a motorcycle while he was on the sidewalk?" Philip shook his head. "Must be the shot they gave him."

Not according to the campus policeman who came to question them. He told them the skid marks showed that Charlie had been hit not by a car, but a motorcycle. "Big one, from the looks of it," he said. "Weird thing was, the marks were on the sidewalk, not the road. Looks to us like that bike came right up on the street after your friend."

When he had gone, Jodie put her hands on her hips and faced her friends. "So, how much more proof do you need?" she said. "Charlie was right about something awful happening to Tanner. That bike came right up on the sidewalk after him. So isn't it obvious that Charlie was deliberately run down on his way to her house because he was going to snoop around, see what he could find out?"

"You don't know that," Sandy said, her face very pale. "You're jumping to conclusions. Maybe some guy on a bike got drunk and couldn't tell where the road ended and the sidewalk began. It happens, Jodie."

Vince agreed with Sandy. "I think you're reaching, Jodie. What are the chances that this has anything to do with Tanner? Pretty remote, right?"

"Oh, absolutely," Jodie said sarcastically. "Let's see, Tanner is missing, and Charlie was run down in her front yard. I'm sure it's just a coincidence."

"You don't even know that Tanner *is* missing," Sandy argued. "I mean, not really *missing*. We're just . . . just not sure exactly where she is, that's all. She could be with her dad in Hawaii or with her mother wherever, we don't know."

Jodie knew that Sandy was so nervous and high-strung she couldn't bear to think about anything bad happening. Sandy sometimes had to take medication for anxiety, so she could concentrate on her studies, and occasionally had bad nightmares that awakened both of them in the middle of the night. To keep herself calm, Sandy worked hard at avoiding unpleasant realities, pushing them away like annoying insects.

"I wish you'd quit being so dramatic." Sandy continued. "You're scaring me."

"Good!" Jodie cried. "Maybe if I scare you, you'll listen to me. I'm making sense, Sandy. We can't just wish this one away, the way you usually do."

"Look," Vince said, "this isn't getting us anywhere. Why don't we try to contact Tanner's dad? That shouldn't be too hard. Someone at Butler Hall will know where he is. And if Tanner's not with him, her father will tell us how to contact her mother, right? That way, when Charlie wakes up, we'll have news for him. We can tell him exactly where Tanner is before he's discharged tomorrow. It'll be good for him."

"*If*," Jodie said darkly, "Tanner really *is* with one of her parents. And I, personally, don't believe that she is."

But she went with them to the administration building, as anxious as the rest of them to get some answers. They were given Dr. Leo's number in Hawaii, and moved out into the lobby to make the call, using Sloane's credit card. He placed the call.

He hung up, disappointment on his handsome face, a minute or so later. "Not at his hotel," he announced glumly. "On another island somewhere, can't be reached. They said he wouldn't be back until tomorrow."

Jodie frowned. "You didn't talk very long. Did you tell them how important it was?"

Sloane glared at her. "Yes, Joellen, I did."

They stood around the telephone, lost in gloom for several minutes before Jodie lifted her head and said, "I think I know why Charlie went to Tanner's house. I think he was planning to break in."

That shocked all of them into open-mouthed stares.

"No, I think he was. Listen . . ." She told them what the campus security officer had said about not beginning an investigation because there was no sign of forced entry at the Tanner house. "So, I think Charlie was planning to fake a break-in and," Jodie added eagerly, "I think it's a great idea. If we go over there and break a window or something, nothing major, just make it look like someone might have been trespassing, the police will investigate. It's the only way we're going to get them to do something before the seventy-two hours is up." She looked at her friends pleadingly. "Seventy-two hours is an awfully long time, guys. Anything could happen to Tanner in seventy-two hours."

"You are *not* breaking into that house, Jodie," Sandy said firmly. "You'll get arrested and get thrown out of school, maybe even sent to jail." She shuddered at the thought.

"No, I won't. If I get caught, I'll just throw myself on the mercy of the police, explain to them that I'm worried sick about Tanner. They'll understand. Anyway, before the police get there I can hunt for a phone number for Tanner's mother, right?"

"Joellen," Sloane warned, shaking his head, "this is too risky. It's crazy. None of us are detectives. And if you *are* right about Charlie trying it first, well, look what happened to him." He waved a hand toward Charlie's cubicle. "You want to end up in here, too? I'm telling you, stay away from that house."

"Well, you guys could come with me," Jodie said innocently. "What are friends for?"

"Not me," Sandy said, shaking her head, her hands up in mock self-defense. "I'm not going near that place. I don't think Tanner is there at all; I think she's with her mother in Bangkok or Hong Kong or Singapore, wherever. Anyway, I'm not playing detective. And you shouldn't be, either, Jodie. You're going to get yourself in a mess of trouble."

Vince said awkwardly, "Look, Jodie, if you really think something has happened to Tanner, you have to let the police handle it. That's what they're for."

Close to tears, Jodie protested, "But they're *not* handling it. They're not doing anything."

"They will," Philip said quietly, patting her shoulder.

Jodie jerked away. "Okay, never mind then! Forget I ever said anything." She began backing away from them, her lips tightly pressed together. "You guys can do whatever you want. I'm going to . . . class."

"Jodie . . ." Philip said softly. "Come on, don't be mad."

But Jodie turned on her heel and, head high, shoulders stiff, hurried down the hall to the exit and disappeared, slamming the door behind her.

Had her friends exited just behind her instead of going back in to check on Charlie one more time before leaving the infirmary, none of the four would have been surprised to see Jodie head not back across campus, but straight toward Faculty Row and Dr. Milton Frederick Leo's brick house.

Chapter 13

Tanner had no sense of passing time as she lay on the floor in the music room. The cuckoo emerged every hour on the hour, but she stopped listening to the shrill sound after a while, uncaring. What difference did it make what time it was, when she wasn't going anywhere? Not to class, not to orchestra practice, not to Vinnie's for pizza or Burgers Etc. for lunch, not to a dance or a movie or the mall. She wasn't leaving this room. Not as long as *he* had anything to say about it.

She knew she must be a horrendous sight. She'd been sweating in that booth, and didn't have a comb. Her hair was matted on her shoulders. Her eyes felt swollen, her feet were streaked with dried blood. They were beginning to hurt and she knew she should check to see how deep the cuts were, but that seemed like far too much effort. Besides, what could she do about it?

I want a bath, she thought fiercely, lying on her stomach, her head resting on her arms. The cuckoo came and went again, but Tanner failed to notice. I want a bath and a shampoo and I want clean clothes, maybe a nice, soft pair of jeans and my new red sweater. Charlie's going to love that sweater. He's crazy about red.

Charlie . . . fresh tears stung Tanner's eyes. She fought them back. How seriously had Charlie been hurt? Was he even . . . was he even alive? Oh, yes, yes, Charlie had to be alive, of course he was. Charlie couldn't be . . . dead. Not possible. Unbearable, thinking of Charlie not being alive. But what had happened to him that put him on that stretcher, in that ambulance? What?

If only she'd been in the music room when it happened, she would have seen the whole thing. But she'd been in the kitchen. Or maybe she'd already come back here by then, but had fallen asleep. Either way, she'd hadn't seen Charlie's accident.

Tanner pushed herself up on her elbows. What was it she'd been doing in the kitchen? Why had Sigmund let her out of the music room? She couldn't remember. Her stomach ached with hunger pangs, so she knew she hadn't eaten. Then why had they gone to the kitchen in the first place? And why couldn't she remember leaving the kitchen to come back here?

Suddenly, she saw the scrap of gaudy, inexpensive fabric covered with flowers in harsh rust and brilliant yellow, waving before her eyes like a flag, teasing, tantalizing, hanging somewhere . . .

Hanging where? Where had she seen that flag of fabric?

Tanner sat up, resting her back against the couch. She remembered the pattern, knew that it was part of an outfit that Silly had made. Why was she thinking of that now? She had barely asked herself the question when the memory returned, flooding back to her, unwelcome as debris brought back in with the tide. She saw it all, in one horrible, vivid image that slammed into Tanner, knocking her backward against the couch, and stealing the breath from her body. She cried out in pain and terror, her hands flying to her mouth, her eyes filled with horror.

That plump, freckled wrist, laden with inexpensive silver bangles, in the freezer, turning bluish-white . . .

Silly hadn't left early. She hadn't left the house at all.

She was still here.

"Oh, God!" Tanner cried, throwing her head back, covering her eyes with her hands, "oh, God, no, not Silly! He wouldn't have, he couldn't have . . ."

But she knew that he had.

And as she cried for the loss of Silly, Tanner knew why, when she had been struggling with Sigmund for control of the freezer lid, it had hit her, suddenly and without explanation, that he was capable of killing. She hadn't seen Silly yet, hadn't known, but some inner, sixth sense had warned her. Had told her the awful, unbelievable truth.

Now she believed it, with all her heart and soul.

He was capable of killing. He had already killed.

And he was coming back.

Why, why, *why*? she screamed silently, and then immediately asked herself if it really mattered why. Did it? Was the reason worth anything? Would it change anything to know why he was doing this? Would it bring Silly back?

No. But a reason would at least keep it from being totally senseless, like those random shootings she sometimes saw on television. They always seemed so much worse than a crime of passion involving jealousy or revenge, because the killer never had any reason. He had just felt like killing. Wasted lives, just because some crazy got his hands on a gun.

But this wasn't that kind of thing, she reminded herself. Because he'd said he knew her father. This was no random attack.

If his anger was toward her father, it didn't seem at all fair that Silly and Tanner, and now Charlie, had been caught in the crossfire.

Tanner swiped at her face with the sleeve of her sweatshirt. How many more people would be hurt before this horrible nightmare was over? And how, exactly, was it going to end?

Charlie had been on his way there to look for her when something had happened to him. Did that mean it hadn't been an accident, after all? Sigmund could have been watching for visitors, and gone out to stop Charlie. Was he going to do that to anyone who came looking for her?

How was she ever going to get out of there?

Resting her head against the back of the couch, Tanner thought despondently how quiet and depressing the house was going to seem without Silly in it, belting out her country songs at the top of her lungs.

Murderer! she thought with fierce rage, clenching and unclenching her hands, digging her nails into her palms until she drew blood.

You're a filthy murderer, Sigmund. Silly never hurt anyone in her entire life. You had no right to kill her. No right, no right . . .

Tears of fury were sliding down her cheeks when she heard the key turning in the lock. A moment later, the door flew open.

Tanner jumped to her feet and faced him, shaking with more rage than fear. She was too angry to be afraid. "You're insane!" she shouted, raising her clenched fists to wave them in his face. "No wonder you knew my father! You're probably the craziest patient he's ever had in his life!"

In two strides he was at her side, gripping her wrist, twisting it painfully, the rubber mask so close, she could see his bared teeth. They were straight and even and very clean. "Don't you ever say anything like that to me again!" he hissed, his breath hot on her skin. "You're a liar, just like your father! I'm not crazy, and I never was. Never, never, *never!*"

"Then let me *go!*" Tanner cried, struggling to free her wrist. "This isn't sane, what you're doing, keeping me a prisoner in my own home, building that stupid coffin, putting me in there. If you want to prove that you're not crazy, stop acting like you are and let me out of here!"

Dropping her wrist, he stepped away from

her. "Oh, I'm afraid I can't do that," he said calmly. "Not just yet. Not until Papa Bear knows what's going on."

"My father? I told you, he can't afford to pay you ransom."

"Who said anything about ransom? I don't need his money. I told you, I just need . . . satisfaction. I just want him to know that I'm in control here. He said I wasn't. Wasn't in control at all, needed someone else to control me, a whole bunch of someone elses. Wrote it down on paper and signed his name." Sigmund shrugged. "I'm just proving him wrong, that's all. Showing all of them just exactly how much control I really do have. You're helping me do it." He tilted his head. "Isn't that nice of you? And ironic, don't you think? That the doctor's own daughter is helping me prove a point."

"All you're doing," Tanner said with contempt, rubbing her aching wrist, "is proving that my father was *right*. Not that he was wrong." And, she added silently, if you can't see that, you're even crazier than my father thought. But she wasn't about to utter those words out loud. After the way he'd reacted a minute ago, accusing him again would only prove her as foolish as he was insane.

Humor him, she thought, humor him.

But she never got the chance.

Taking his attention away from her, his eyes swept the room.

Tanner watched in astonishment then as his body tensed and his mouth behind the mask tightened and he began striding back and forth in the area near the grand piano, cursing and shouting. "Look at this mess! What the hell have you been doing in here, young lady? This is disgusting. Glass everywhere, you've broken a perfectly good lamp, and these bloodstains will never come out. This beautiful carpet is ruined, just ruined!"

Tanner couldn't believe what she was seeing and hearing. This . . . maniacal creature in a grotesque Halloween mask was marching back and forth in her father's music room, sounding just like her father, and looking like him, in spite of the mask. There was a definite resemblance in the way he marched back and forth, shoulders and spine aligned perfectly, like a wooden soldier. Her father did that when some political issue had made him angry. He waved his arms and shouted, just as Sigmund was doing now.

The resemblance was eerie.

"This isn't even your house," Tanner said indignantly. "What do you care what happens to it?"

His head came up. He stopped pacing and raced across the room to her. Grabbing her elbow, he screamed into her face, "How dare you speak to me like that? You have no manners, miss! None whatsoever! You need to be taught a lesson."

And then, to her horror, he was grasping the neck of her sweatshirt and dragging her straight toward The Booth again.

"No!" she screamed, struggling, fighting him, kicking out with her bloodied feet. "No, don't put me in there again, I can't stand it, please, I'll behave, I promise, just don't put me in there!" She hated the pleading in her voice, but she hated even more the thought of that dark, airless space. And once inside, she would have no chance, none at all, of escaping him.

"This is for your own good," he said grimly, not easing his grip on her elbow or her sweatshirt. "You must learn your lesson. We have rules around here, and you have to follow them the same as everyone else. One bad apple can spoil the bunch, you know. If we let you get away with things, we'll have to let others do the same, and then where will we be? Take your punishment like a man, and your character will be the better for it."

Later, Tanner would remember those words and realize that they weren't really his words.

He'd been parroting someone else. Someone in authority, someone in control. He was repeating what, sometime, somewhere, had been told to him.

But for now, all Tanner could do was kick and scream and fight with what little strength she had left, trying to save herself from The Booth.

In vain.

She fought valiantly, but she hadn't eaten anything in too long, and the shock of what had happened to Charlie and Silly had drained her both emotionally and physically. She had so little strength left.

He, on the other hand, seemed as strong as an ox.

In a matter of minutes, Tanner was dumped into The Booth like a sack of laundry, the door was slammed shut against her, and she heard the heavy chunk of wood twisting into place.

"And you'll stay there until you develop some manners, Miss!" he shouted.

Tanner sat in a lump on the floor, slumped against the rear wall of The Booth, legs bent at the knee, her hands in her lap, listening for the sound of his departure.

It didn't come right away.

In her darkness, she heard him moving around in the music room, heard him muttering angrily to himself, heard pieces of glass clinking against each other, realized that he was probably cleaning up her mess. Insane . . . he really was insane.

She went over, in her head, the words he'd said when he was dragging her to The Booth. And she realized that the words had sounded like something that would be said by the head of a school, maybe a strict private school, or a summer camp or a . . . hospital. Not a regular hospital, where you went to mend broken bones, to have surgery, to cure an illness. Not that kind. The other kind.

Sigmund knew her father.

Her father was a doctor.

A doctor of psychiatry.

When he sent someone to a hospital, he sent them to the *other* kind. There were, she knew, residential treatment centers for people their age with mental or emotional problems. She knew because her father sometimes visited them, and often received mail from them. They dealt with behavioral disorders as well as emotional problems, and some might well use a treatment like The Booth for more difficult cases. "Time out," Sigmund had called it. Yes, that might be something that would be used in the kind of place she was thinking about.

Was that why he was so angry? Because her

father had sent him to one of those places?

Tanner glanced fearfully around her hated prison. Well, if Sigmund had spent a lot of time in a place just like this one, she almost couldn't blame him for being angry. Being in this tiny, airless space was enough to drive even the sanest person insane.

Chapter 14

The cuckoo clock only struck once while Tanner was crouched on the floor of The Booth, but it felt to her as if she'd been in there forever. By the time he let her out, she was thoroughly subdued. All the fight had been drained out of her by her struggle inside that awful box. The struggle was twofold: first, to breathe properly in spite of the lack of air, and second, to hang on to her sanity. The second was by far the more difficult of the two.

The skylight above her had gone dark. Either night had fallen or the weather had become more severe. Tanner didn't really care. What difference did it make what was going on outside? She wasn't a part of it.

Maybe she never would be again.

"I'm going to let you out," Sigmund warned as he held the door to the booth open, "but if you break or even bend one of the rules, you'll be back in The Booth so fast, you'll see stars."

"I don't even know what the rules are," Tanner muttered sullenly. Taking deep breaths of air, she moved quickly away from him to take a seat on the couch. Her feet hurt when she walked, and she knew she should look at them, maybe wash them off in the tiny sink in the lavatory. For now, all she wanted to do was breathe.

He took a seat opposite her, in the leather chair. Crossed his legs, just like her father did.

"No more throwing stuff at the windows," he said. "I'm not cleaning up any more of your messes."

Of course he'd figured out how the lamp and candy dish had been broken. He wasn't stupid. Just crazy.

"I'm hungry," Tanner complained in that same, truculent voice. "I haven't had anything to eat since yesterday at noon. Is that how you intend to get your stupid satisfaction, by starving me to death?"

"I'm not going to starve you. I'll get you a sandwich." He stood up. The ugly mask looked down at her sternly. "I don't have to lock you in The Booth while I'm gone, do I?"

She shook her head. "No. I don't have the energy to do anything brave." That was the truth.

Nodding, he left. The key turned in the lock a moment later.

Tanner let her head rest against the back of the couch. She felt like she'd been swimming through tar. So weak, so tired. How was she going to fight him?

Her eyes went to the screens high on the walls. Nothing out front, just the gray mist of rain, still falling steadily. She could hear it tap-tapping against the skylight, a rhythm as steady as the ticking of a clock. Her eyes went to the screen monitoring the backyard, and there she saw movement.

Tanner sat up. A figure, darting in and out among the bushes and trees, there, behind the gazebo!

She rubbed her eyes. Maybe she'd imagined it. Maybe she wanted so desperately to believe that someone had come to rescue her that she was having hallucinations.

No, there it was again, stealthily creeping from bush to bush.

Rain hat, slicker . . . could be anyone. Charlie? No. Charlie was hurt. Couldn't be Charlie.

Light from one of the windows bounced off a pair of eyeglasses.

Eyeglasses. Jodie? It was Jodie, lurking about out there in the shadows? Jodie had come to see why it was that Tanner Leo wasn't attending classes, wasn't at orchestra practice, wasn't anywhere to be seen on campus?

So Jodie hadn't believed the note.

Tanner's heart lurched. Charlie hadn't either, and he had suffered dearly for it!

Be careful, Jodie, she warned silently, her spine stiffening as her eyes remained focused on the screen. He's here, Jodie, he's here, in the kitchen, and if he sees you . . .

Jodie would be careful. She was smart, clever. Smarter than any of the rest of them.

What was Jodie doing out there in the backyard alone? Why weren't Vince and Philip with her? Where were Sandy and Sloane? They should never have let Jodie come there alone.

But then, they couldn't know that something was very, very wrong in this house, could they? Because Sigmund had put that note on the mailbox. As far as her friends were concerned, she was off in the Orient with her mother.

Well, Charlie hadn't bought that. And apparently, Jodie hadn't either, or she wouldn't be slinking around in the backyard.

The key turned in the lock, and Tanner jumped guiltily. She would have to be very, very careful to keep her eyes away from that screen. If he caught her looking up there, he'd see what she was seeing. He'd see Jodie.

Tanner shuddered. She would *not* look up at that screen.

If only there was some way she could warn Jodie.

But there wasn't.

All he brought her was a sandwich, two pieces of bread slapped together with a thin slice of cold meat in the middle. No lettuce, no tomato, no chips, not even any mustard, and nothing to drink.

But maybe that was better. If she ate very quickly, maybe he'd leave. And Jodie would be safe.

He thrust the plate at her. "Hurry up!" he demanded, sitting back down in the leather chair. He didn't glance up at the screen, didn't even seem aware of it. "I have places to go, things to do. I don't want to attract attention by not being there. People ask too many questions, that's one thing I've learned."

"Are you wearing that disgusting mask because I'd recognize you?" Tanner asked abruptly. "Why else would you wear it? Although," she added with contempt, "I can't imagine that someone who's doing what you're doing could be someone I actually *know*."

"Maybe I just don't want you describing me for some clever police artist when all of this is over," he said.

Hope sprang to life in Tanner's chest. That sounded like he wasn't going to kill her, after all.

That hope was dashed immediately when he added slyly, "Or the mask could be because of what you said. Could be that you'd recognize me. Who knows? Just hurry up and eat, okay? I'm late already."

Tanner chewed hastily. He had places to go, things to do? His absence would be missed? Did that mean he was a student with a busy schedule? Her father treated students. But then, he treated people in Twin Falls, too.

"If my father did something to you," she said through a mouthful of sandwich, "why don't you wait until he comes back and deal with him? Why me?"

"Don't talk with your mouth full," he reprimanded sharply, "or you'll end up back in The Booth."

Tanner submitted, finishing the sandwich in two huge bites. She could barely swallow, there was such a lump of fear in her throat for Jodie. Suppose he decided to check the backyard before he left?

She was dying of thirst, but was afraid to send him back to the kitchen. The windows in there overlooked the backyard. She would have to wait, get a drink from the tiny sink in the lavatory after he'd gone.

"I'm outa here," he said brusquely when she'd finished. "I'm leaving you out of The Booth, but I could come back at any time and check on you. If one single thing is out of place in this room, you'll be spending the rest of the night in there, and that's a promise."

"I'm just going to go to sleep," she said, feigning a yawn. "I'm tired." Maybe if he thought she was sleepy, he'd leave more quickly. Without checking out back.

Instinctively, before she could stop herself, Tanner's eyes rose to the screen. There, the rain hat moved behind a bench near the rose garden.

She felt his eyes on her, and quickly averted her gaze. She shouldn't have looked. A terrible mistake, after promising herself that she wouldn't while he was in the room. Had he noticed? Had he seen anything moving on the screen?

She couldn't tell. He didn't seem to be looking at it now. But . . . God, what a careless fool she was!

Maybe he hadn't noticed.

"I'm not saying when I'll be back," he said, taking the empty plate from her hands. "You just better stay where you are, because I could walk in here at any time."

"You said you'd get me a blanket," she reminded him. It was already getting cold in the room.

"Changed my mind," he answered callously. "Don't have time to go hunting for one. Not that cold in here, anyway."

"It is too."

"No, it's not. Besides, adversity is good for your character. I'd spoil you by giving you a blanket. Spoiling isn't good for people. It ruins them. You should learn that life isn't all cozy warmth. Might as well learn it now."

He was quoting again, she was sure. People their age never said adversity was good for character, except as a joke. He wasn't joking.

The second he had left the room and the key had clicked in the lock, Tanner jumped up, her eyes flying to the backyard screen. Nothing. She saw nothing but the gardens and the benches and the gazebo and the trees.

Her heart sank. Had Jodie given up? Gone back to campus without checking out the house?

No . . . there, on the other side of the patio, behind the gingko tree, an arm.

Tanner exhaled. Jodie was still here. And

he'd gone. Now, if Jodie could only find a way into the house.

It was maddening not to be able to hear anything. Not the front door closing, proving that he really had left the house, not Jodie's voice if she shouted Tanner's name, nothing.

She glanced up at the front yard screen. There was nothing there now but the trees, the broken picket fence, and a dark, deserted, rainy Faculty Row.

When her eyes switched quickly back to the other screen, there was Jodie, hurrying through the rain to the back porch.

She must have heard Sigmund leave, or she wouldn't be approaching the house.

That was reassuring.

To Tanner's complete astonishment, when Jodie put her hand on the back doorknob, it turned and the door opened.

He'd left the back door unlocked?

Maybe it had never *been* locked, and he hadn't ever bothered to check. Knowing how paranoid her father was, Sigmund might have just assumed everything was locked. But Silly would have been in and out of that door a dozen times yesterday, not intending to lock it for the final time until she was ready to leave for the day.

But she had never left for the day. So the back door had remained unlocked.

Silly . . .

Tanner fought back tears. It was Jodie she should be thinking about now, not Silly.

Once Jodie was inside the house, Tanner could no longer see her. She didn't know what to do. Screaming and shouting wouldn't do any good. But pounding on the door might. Sound-proofing wouldn't silence the sound of fists hammering on wood, would it? If a tree falls in the forest . . .

Tanner shook herself. Get a grip! she ordered. This may be your one chance to save yourself from this nightmare.

She ran to the door with every intention of pounding to attract Jodie's attention. But both hands were still so bruised and swollen from banging on the front wall earlier that day that the slightest touch on the heavy wooden door sent arrows of pain up her arms, making her feel sick and faint. She couldn't pass out now, not when help was so close at hand.

She couldn't kick the door, either, with her feet lacerated.

The blows that she finally gave the door were more like pats, gentle slaps, the only pressure she could manage with her hands so sore.

Maybe Jodie would somehow, miraculously, hear her tapping.

She slapped against the door for what seemed like hours. She was about to give up when there was a whispering sound beneath her feet. When she looked down, a small piece of white paper was sliding underneath the door. Gasping, Tanner bent and snatched it off the floor.

The writing on the notepaper was Jodie's. It read, simply, *Tanner? Are you in there?*

"Oh, God," Tanner sobbed gratefully, slumping against the door awash with relief. Finally! Finally, someone had found her!

She was about to be saved.

Chapter 15

Jodie was as surprised as Tanner to find the back door unlocked.

She had been waiting in the backyard, hiding behind a tree, trying to decide what to do, when she heard someone leave the house by the side door next to the driveway. Although she had rushed to that side of the house, she had only seen enough of the figure departing through the dark and the rain to realize that it definitely wasn't Tanner. And there was something very weird about it, something about the head, but Jodie couldn't tell what it was exactly. Maybe he was wearing a funny kind of rain hat.

Jodie was pretty sure of two things. It had looked like a guy, and it *wasn't* Tanner's father. So what was he doing in Tanner's house? He couldn't be burglarizing it. He'd have to have a car or van for that, and she didn't see one.

He'd taken off on foot. How much could you steal on foot?

Jodie's skin crawled. What was a stranger doing in Tanner's house?

There was only one way to find out. She would have to go inside.

If all the doors were locked, she'd break a window, as Charlie had suggested.

But all the doors weren't locked. When Jodie sneaked up onto the porch and turned the doorknob, her mouth fell open with surprise as it turned easily and the door opened. If Tanner really had gone off to the Orient or whatever, she never would have left a door unlocked.

Jodie pulled the door open and peered inside. Except for a piece of material hanging over the edge of the freezer, nothing looked weird. The back porch and the kitchen were clean, and empty.

Maybe Tanner was sick. Maybe she was upstairs, so sick that she couldn't answer the phone or the doorbell, couldn't even call a doctor. There were probably rare, exotic fevers that did that sometimes. It would be awful if Tanner had been sick all this time and they hadn't even known it.

Quietly, the way one does in a silent house, Jodie closed the door and moved on into the kitchen, walking cautiously, as if she expected someone to jump out from behind a door at any second.

There was a small lamp on in the dining room to her right, another in the living room at the front of the house, also on her right, and a light shining from the hall upstairs. Dr. Leo was apparently willing to pay an expensive electricity bill in order to fool burglars. Jodie was grateful. Bad enough creeping around in someone else's house, without having to do it in the pitch-dark.

She went upstairs first, hoping as she opened Tanner's bedroom door that she would find Tanner lying under the covers, maybe with a box of tissues and a bottle of aspirin at her side.

But the bed, neatly made, was empty.

Jodie sagged against the doorframe. If Tanner *were* here, this was where she would be. A serious illness was the only thing that would have kept Tanner from Charlie's side after the accident, that is, if Tanner were still in the area.

Clearly, she wasn't.

The note hadn't been a joke.

At least, now they knew. But, Jodie thought miserably, how am I ever going to break this to Charlie? He was so sure Tanner wouldn't go off and leave him, not without calling first. He'd be devastated.

But Tanner wouldn't have, Jodie heard him saying, and she knew, in spite of evidence to the contrary, that he was right.

Moving swiftly and surely, Jodie left the doorway to move to the double closet along one wall. She pulled the folding doors open.

The closet was full. There wasn't a bare hanger anywhere in sight. The upper shelves were crammed full of heavy sweaters, the carpeted floor littered with shoes.

Clamping her lips tightly together, Jodie whirled and ran to the triple dresser along the opposite wall.

The drawers, like the closet, were full. Lingerie, T-shirts, pajamas, sweatsuits, scarves, not a single drawer had so much as a dent in the piles of clothing.

As if that hadn't told Jodie the whole story, a framed picture of Charlie, grinning widely, sat on the dresser. Jodie glanced over at the bedside table. Another picture, this one of Charlie and Tanner together, both in shorts and Salem University T-shirts, standing on the riverbank behind school, their arms around each other. Both were smiling.

Jodie leaned against the dresser. Tanner had

said in her note, "See you next fall." Who packed for months in the Orient or anywhere else for that matter without making a dent in closet or drawers?

And Tanner would never, *never* have gone off and left these pictures behind. Not in a million years.

Jodie turned and ran lightly down the stairs, then stood, perplexed, in the hall. What to do? Call the police? Call Charlie? No, he was in the infirmary. He might have a relapse or something when she told him he'd definitely been right.

The noise Jodie heard then was so soft, so muted, she wasn't sure she'd actually heard anything. A faint slapping sound, waves against a shore, someone smacking at a pesky fly, a piece of paper flapping in the wind? Like that. An insignificant sound, nothing that told her anything important.

But it came again, and then a third time.

From somewhere off to her left.

Jodie turned. The music room. The room Tanner hated. Completely soundproofed, one of the reasons Tanner hated it. "It was like the rest of the world had disappeared when I was in there," she'd said. "I've never felt that alone anywhere else."

Jodie reached out to try the doorknob. Locked. But the faint slapping sound came again. It was coming from behind the door, she was sure of it.

Jodie moved closer. If someone screamed or yelled or shouted from inside that room, would they be heard from outside? Did soundproof really mean exactly that? That not a single sound could escape those four walls?

What about if you were inside? Could someone inside that room hear sounds from the outside?

Probably not.

"Tanner?" she said softly, and then, realizing how foolish that was, said it louder. "Tanner?"

No answer.

And the slapping sound had stopped.

Nothing but silence.

But Jodie was like a dog with a bone now. The closets upstairs, still full, the drawers, still packed with Tanner's clothes, the photographs of Charlie, had convinced her that Tanner had never left this house. And there *had* been a sound, no matter how small, from inside the music room.

She thought deeply for several minutes. Then she turned and ran to the small telephone table in the hall, found a notepad and a pen, and scribbled a hurried message. Just a few words. But if she was right, those few words would be enough.

Her heart was pounding like a tom-tom as she slid the piece of paper under the door. The threshold was sealed so tightly, she was sure for a second or two that even something as skinny as that piece of paper wouldn't slide through. But she kept pushing, and finally, it slid free of her hands.

Then Jodie waited.

On the other side of the door, Tanner picked up the note and read it. And rejoiced.

Jodie hadn't even signed it. But it didn't matter. The note, brief though it was, was enough. Someone had found her!

But she was wasting time, reveling in the joy of having been found. She had to answer the note quickly, before Jodie decided the house was empty, after all.

Tanner ran to her father's desk. It smelled of lemon oil. But this was not a man who kept piles of letters and magazines and bills scattered across his furniture. There was not a piece of paper anywhere in sight. There was a paisley cup filled with newly sharpened pencils, a matching blotter, a framed photograph of Tanner from tenth grade, a heavy metal ruler, an expensive gold pen in a holder, a brass business card holder boasting a neat stack of crisp white cards bearing Dr. Leo's name and profession, and a large Scotch tape dispenser. But there was not a single piece of paper.

Muttering under her breath, "Neat freak, neat freak!" Tanner grasped at the center drawer's brass handle and gave it a tug. Locked. Of course. They were probably all locked up tighter than a penitentiary.

They were.

Gasping in frustration, Tanner's eyes darted about the room. There had to be a piece of paper somewhere in this room.

The piano bench. The lid lifted, and underneath that lid there were stacks of sheet music, maybe even some music composition books.

Tanner ran. Jerked the lid upward. Grabbed the first piece of sheet music she saw. Then she ran back to her father's desk and yanked the gold pen from its holder to scribble, *I'm here! Help! T.* across the top.

Back in front of the door, she threw herself to the floor, lying on her stomach as she pushed the sheet music into the tiny crack beneath the door.

It didn't fit.

Too thick.

She pushed and pushed, sobbing with frustration, but the top edge of the sheet caught, crumpled, and refused to move. Desperate, she pushed harder, but all that did was crumple the bottom half of the sheet as well, until what she was holding in her hand looked like a used napkin.

"Oh, God," Tanner whispered, and scrambled to her feet. All of the sheet music was the same texture, the same thickness. No good, no good . . .

The lavatory . . . the stack of paper towels . . . would one of those be thin enough?

"Don't leave, Jodie," she whispered frantically, "don't leave, not yet! I'm coming, I'm coming!"

She didn't even feel the pain in her feet as she dashed across the carpet to the lavatory, threw herself inside, clutched a handful of towels to her chest and ran back to the door again, where the gold pen lay waiting.

Scribbling the same message, whispering, "Don't leave, Jodie, don't give up and leave!" Tanner thrust the paper towel under the door.

It stuck . . . but just for a moment, and then Tanner sagged in relief as the towel disappeared from sight.

In the hallway, Jodie, crouched beside the door, stared as the waffled piece of paper edged its way toward her. Grinning with glee, she snatched it up and read it. And shouted for joy,

"Tanner! Tanner, that's you? You're in there? Hallelujah! We *knew* you hadn't deserted us, we knew it, Charlie and I."

Tanner, lying with her ear pressed against the tiny crack at the bottom of the door, heard Jodie's words. They were faint, but discernible, and they felt like drops of water after a long thirst. Another human voice . . . not *his*, not Sigmund's! She felt a rush of warmth for Jodie. It had been very brave of her to come into this house alone.

"Is Charlie okay?" she whispered into the tiny gap, and then realized that Jodie certainly couldn't hear her if she whispered, so she repeated the question, this time in a shout.

Jodie had to kneel next to the door to make herself heard. "Yes!" she cried, her lips pressing into the wood. "Yes, he is! How can I get you out of there? Where's the key?"

"*He* has it!"

"He?" Until then, Jodie hadn't really thought about *how* Tanner had become trapped in the music room. But if she had thought about it, she would have assumed it was accidental, an oversight on Tanner's part somehow.

The words "*he* has it" changed the picture completely. It stunned Jodie. She hadn't thought, hadn't let herself think, as Charlie had, that something criminal had happened to

Tanner. But that figure she'd seen leaving the house . . . that must be the "he."

Why would someone want to keep Tanner a prisoner in this house?

"Is there another key?" Jodie called out.

"No, I don't think so, I don't know. Jodie, get me *out* of here! He's crazy!"

"Let me look for another key. Hold tight, Tanner, I'll be right back." Jodie searched the hallway, checking under the stair treads, over the doorframe, in the brass umbrella stand near the front door. Nothing. No sign of a key.

She hurried into the kitchen, hunting for a key rack. They had one at home, back in Buffalo, in the shape of a big, fat, black and white cow. Her father had nailed it on the wall next to the refrigerator.

There was a bulletin board in the kitchen, but no key rack. Jodie went on into the back porch. There could be a key rack by the back door.

There wasn't.

If she had to, she could take the door off the hinges. She'd seen her mother do it more than once when one of her younger brothers or sisters had locked themselves in the bathroom. All she needed was a screwdriver or putty knife and a hammer.

She glanced around the small, knotty pine-paneled porch for some sign of tools, murmuring, "I'm going to get you out of there, I promise!"

And a voice from behind her said lightly, "Guess again."

Chapter 16

In the music room, still lying with her face pressed up against the door, Tanner called anxiously, "Jodie? Jodie? Are you still there?"

Something was wrong.

Something had happened. Something bad. Jodie had been gone too long. She would have been back by now if something hadn't happened.

Tanner, her eyes filled with dread, pushed herself to a sitting position beside the door. No, no, no! She'd been so close! So close to getting out. What had happened? Was *he* back? Had he found Jodie going through the house, searching for the key?

What had he done to Jodie?

In despair, Tanner opened her mouth and screamed Jodie's name repeatedly until her throat was raw. She didn't care if *he* heard. What did it matter? He wasn't going to let her go, anyway, no matter how cooperative she was. He had never intended to let her go, she knew that now. The mask was just a way of tormenting her, letting her think she'd be alive to identify him.

The sound of her anguished screams for Jodie rocked the music room.

When she was too drained to make another sound, she sat up. She had to do something. If he was in the house, he'd be here, any second now. He'd toss her into that coffin, bar the door, and she'd be helpless again.

No! She wasn't going to be helpless again, not this time.

She jumped up and ran to the desk. There had to be something there that would be useful. Something, anything.

The key turned in the lock.

Tanner grabbed the heavy metal ruler and the heavier tape dispenser and tossed them hastily into a dark corner of the coffin. She had no idea what she would do with them, but she wasn't going in there empty-handed again. Then she threw herself onto the couch. Suddenly, the door flew open and *he* stood there, still wearing the mask. Not Jodie, come to save her. *Him.*

Angry. He was angry. He slammed the door behind him and turned to face her, hands on his jeaned hips. "How did you do it?" he shouted, glaring down at her. "How did you contact that girl? How did you get her over here?"

"I . . . I didn't," Tanner protested. "How could I? You took the telephone. She just didn't believe the note you made me write, that's all. She came on her own to check out the house. Where is she? What have you done with her?"

"None of your business." He reached down and grabbed Tanner's shoulder. "Get up! You know the rules. No visitors until you've been here six weeks! Who do you think you are, Queen Elizabeth? You will follow the rules like everyone else in this establishment or I'll know the reason why, young lady."

Before she could jump to her feet as ordered, he began dragging her across the floor toward The Booth. "I didn't *have* visitors," she shouted, arms and legs flailing in an effort to slow him down. "I told you, she came on her own."

"That's right, blame someone else. You're all alike, all of you. Unwilling to accept responsibility for your own actions. That's what got you into this place to begin with. When are you going to learn that there is a consequence for every action? And learn to think before you act? Well, that's what we're here to teach you, miss."

He was quoting again, she could tell. Someone else had said those same things to him, sometime, somewhere. The words had made him angry. And now *she* was paying for that anger.

Her fear for Jodie's safety and her own terror of The Booth sent her babbling, "Please, please, no, no, not in there, don't put me in there, don't!" And then, when he ignored her, continuing to drag her ever closer to the hated box, anger took over and she shouted, "Get your hands off me, you creep! I'm not going in there, I'm *not*!" She was still shouting, "I'm *not*!" and kicking wildly when he grabbed her up off the floor by the neck of her sweatshirt and tossed her into The Booth. The bare sole of her left foot, in mid-kick, slammed into the rough wooden door as it closed, reopening the cuts made earlier by the fragments of glass.

Tanner cried out in pain and despair and frustration, and would have pounded against the door if her hands hadn't been so sore.

"You're spending the night in there!" Sigmund shouted as the latch twisted into place. "We'll see if that doesn't teach you to obey the rules."

"Don't leave me in here!" Tanner cried, her face pressed against the door, "don't! I can't stand it, not all night, please, let me out!"

But the next sound she heard was the music room door closing, the key turning with an angry click.

She was alone again.

Chapter 17

For long minutes after the key turned in the music room door, Tanner sat on the floor of the coffin, her head in her hands. To come so close to being released only to find herself back in the box again was more than she could bear.

And she was heartsick about Jodie. What had Sigmund done to her? Where was she? Was she still alive?

Tanner had never felt so helpless. If Jodie was still alive, somewhere in the house, she had to need help. And Tanner couldn't give it to her. She couldn't even help herself.

The thought of spending the whole night in the dark, suffocating box made her hands shake with terror. Hours and hours and hours . . . it would be like being buried alive. She would never make it through the night without losing her sanity.

Something on the floor was jutting into

Tanner's hip, as if she were carrying something unwieldy in her sweatpants pocket. The tape dispenser. She shifted uncomfortably, remembering then that she had tossed the metal ruler and the dispenser into a corner. Now, lost in her fear for Jodie's safety and her dread of the long hours ahead, she couldn't imagine why she'd done it. What good were they?

Tanner shook her head to clear it. She tried to concentrate. Jodie would have said, "No good sitting on the floor thinking life stinks. *Deal* with it, Tanner!"

Maybe . . . maybe she could use the ruler as a pry bar, inserting it into those small gaps at the corners of The Booth. If it worked, she might be able to separate the back wall from the sides. It was worth a try. And the tape dispenser, heavy as it was, could substitute for a hammer.

She pulled herself to her feet. She wasn't doing Jodie or herself any good by crouching on the floor of this horrid booth feeling sorry for herself. Even if her idea didn't work, the night would pass more quickly if she had something to occupy her time.

Ruler in hand, Tanner hesitated. If Sigmund came in and caught her ripping away at the nails he'd hammered in, he'd be even angrier than he was now.

She laughed at herself for the thought. The guy was planning to *kill* her! So what difference did it make how much angrier he got? What did she have to lose?

Biting her lower lip in fierce concentration, she inserted the metal ruler into one of the gaps along a corner where the back wall met the left side wall. Sliding the ruler down until it was midway between two nails, she pushed against the heavy measuring stick, trying to force the back section away from the side wall.

The gap opened slightly.

But as soon as she pulled the ruler out, the gap closed again.

She understood then, with sinking heart, that her only hope was to somehow remove the nails. She had to use the ruler as a pry bar to pull the nails out of the wood.

That would take her years.

She didn't *have* years. She only had tonight. And maybe not even the entire night. *He* could come back at any time, without warning.

The soles of her feet, bare on the rough wooden floor, were hurting terribly, as if she were standing on a bed of Sigmund's nails. Her head ached from lack of fresh air, and she had to use her sore, swollen hands to feel in the dark for the exact location of the nails.

Grimacing in pain as her bruised hand

gripped the sharp edge of the metal ruler, she inserted it again into a gap, this time sliding it down until it was directly beside a nail. Then she pried the back wall away from the side wall, refusing to ease the pressure until she felt the nail give a little. When it finally did, she forced the edge of the ruler further into the gap, continuing to apply pressure to the ruler. Then she pushed with her shoulder against the back wall, praying the box wouldn't tip over, sending her crashing to the ground.

Slowly, so slowly she thought she would scream with frustration, the nail eased out of its hole in the side wall. It remained fixed in the back wall, pointing toward Tanner, which she decided might be useful. If Sigmund should return unexpectedly, having the nails in place would make it easier for her to close the gaps again temporarily. As long as he didn't inspect it, it might fool the eye.

While she worked, feeling in the dark for the next nail, and the next, she tried to listen for the cuckoo clock's chirp. She ought to keep track of the time. Wishing she'd brought a pen or pencil into the booth with her to scratch the number of passing hours on the wall, she decided instead to use her toes to count. Each time the cuckoo clock chirped the hour, she would snap a piece of transparent tape off the dispenser and wind it around one toe. Ten toes, ten hours. Sigmund probably wouldn't be gone much longer than that. If he was, she'd remove the pieces of tape and start all over again, adding those numbers to the ten she'd already counted.

By the time she had wrapped two of her toes with tape, she had only managed to free two nails. The realization was depressing. One an hour? There had to be at least twenty nails going up one side of the back wall and twenty more down the other side. Forty hours worth of work? She wasn't going to get out of this booth tonight.

Panic flooded her. "I want *out* of here!" she screamed into the deathly silence, slapping the ruler against the back wall and pounding one foot on the floor. Pain like hot lava seared her from the sole of her foot all the way up to her hip, and this time when she screamed, it was agony, not panic, that filled the air.

She couldn't stand on the foot another second. Giving up, she sank to the floor of The Booth, wrapped the bottom of her sweatpants around the throbbing foot, and rested her head against a side wall.

Pain and fear and exhaustion took over then,

and within minutes, against her will, Tanner was asleep.

At the infirmary, Charlie Cochran was not asleep. He was wide awake in his bed, a telephone pressed to his ear. "I don't care about the time difference," he said urgently. "This is an emergency. I need to get in touch with Dr. Leo now. Why can't you give me a number where he can be reached? Inaccessible? What does that mean? If one of his patients was threatening to commit suicide, I bet he'd be accessible, wouldn't he? Well, this is even worse than that. His daughter is missing."

Charlie listened for a minute, then said, "No, I'm not the police. But this is urgent!" Another minute passed, then Charlie said in desperation, "Well, can you tell me how to reach his wife? Ex-wife? Mrs. Leo? Only that's not her name anymore." Charlie searched his memory frantically. What was Tanner's mother's last name? It wasn't Leo. "You're telling me it doesn't make any difference what her name is because you still wouldn't know how to get in touch with her? Great! Thanks for nothing!"

He slammed the phone down angrily.

A nurse came bustling in, carrying a small plastic package from which she removed an object. "What's all the ruckus in here? It's late and you're supposed to be sleeping. You're suffering from trauma, young man. Rest and quiet, that's what the doctor ordered."

The telephone at Charlie's elbow rang. While the nurse busied herself with the package and looked on in disapproval, Charlie grabbed the receiver.

"Charlie?" Sandy's voice. "I didn't wake you up, did I? Is Jodie there?"

"No, I wasn't asleep. How can I sleep when I don't know where Tanner is? I haven't been able to get in touch with her father, and I don't have any idea where her mother is. And no, Jodie isn't here. Why?"

Sandy sounded uncertain. "Well, she wanted to go back to Tanner's, and we all said no, that wasn't a good idea. I mean, what's the point? And we were afraid she'd get into trouble, so we talked her out of it. None of us has seen her since then. I had a newspaper meeting, and then I had a date, so I just got back a little while ago. She's not here. It's pretty late for her to be out. I mean, it's not like she had a date or anything. So I just wondered if she was with you."

"No, she's not." Charlie's voice hardened. "And if I were you, I'd find her. If there's anything we don't need, it's another person missing. Maybe she's with Vince or Philip."

"Uh-uh. Philip checked the library for me, said she wasn't there. Vince wasn't home, even though I'm sure he told me he wasn't going out tonight, but he called me back later and said he hadn't seen her. Sloane hasn't called me back yet, but I'm sure she's not with him. Why would she be? She doesn't like Sloane."

Charlie's bruised face turned grim. "I'm coming over there. They can't keep me here against my will," he said, glowering at the nurse. "I'm going crazy in here not knowing where Tanner is, anyway. We can look for both of them at the same time."

But before he could reach for his clothes, the nurse said, "Oh, I don't think you're going anywhere just now," and Charlie felt a pinprick in his left arm. "Doctor's orders," the nurse repeated cheerfully. "Whatever problem you were about to solve, it'll still be there in the morning. They don't disappear overnight, I'm afraid."

Still holding the telephone, Charlie shouted at her, "You had no right to do that without my permission!"

"I don't need *your* permission," she said matter-of-factly. "Only the doctor's, and I had that. That shot will put you to sleep and in the morning you'll be good as new."

Ignoring Charlie's obvious fury, she left,

turning off the light in his cubicle as she closed the door.

"Oh, God, Sandy, she gave me a shot," Charlie groaned. "I didn't even see it coming. Now I can't leave. Even if I made it over there, I'd be so groggy by the time I got there, I'd be no help at all. I think you should call the police."

"Charlie. You know what they said. Seventy-two hours."

"I don't *care* what they said! I'm stuck in here, and now you tell me Jodie isn't where she's supposed to be, either. Something is very wrong, Sandy. And I have this really lousy feeling that Jodie did go back to the house, after all. You know her. She's like Tanner that way. If Jodie was determined to check that place out again, you guys couldn't keep her away." Charlie could feel the medication beginning to kick in. He struggled to remain alert. "I think you should get the guys and go back over there."

Sandy's voice took on a petulant note. "Charlie, it's late, and it's raining. I got soaked so many times today, I feel like a duck. Anyway, I don't think Jodie would go over there all by herself. She would have bullied all of us into going with her."

"Well, then, where is she?" Charlie demanded.

"Maybe she stayed with a friend tonight," Sandy said, forcing false brightness into her voice. "Yeah, I'll bet she did. She's just having a sleepover with someone. I haven't seen her, so she couldn't tell me about it, that's all."

Charlie's lids felt heavy. But he was so afraid, so afraid for both Tanner and Jodie. He knew Jodie. Going back to the Leo house was exactly the kind of thing she would do. He was convinced that something bad had happened to Tanner in that house, convinced that she had never left it. And now Jodie . . .

"Call around," he said, his words beginning to slur slightly. "Call every friend of Jodie's that you know. And . . . and if she isn't with any of them . . . Sandy . . . you have . . . to call the police. You *have* to. Don't pretend nothing's wrong here, because something *is*."

"Okay, Charlie, okay. I'm really beat, and I think I'm coming down with a cold. My throat feels all scratchy. But if you're going to worry, I'll make the calls, even though I, personally, am absolutely sure that Jodie is just staying with a friend."

"And if she's not . . . if she's not," Charlie murmured drowsily, as his head filled up with wet wool, "you'll call . . . you'll call . . ." Who was it he wanted Sandy to call? The police.

"You'll call the police, right, if she's not with a friend? Sandy?"

"If you say so, Charlie. Go to sleep now. I'll handle it."

When she had hung up, Charlie struggled valiantly to stay awake. But the medication was strong and he was helpless against it.

The worst part was, he knew that he was going to slide into sleep knowing that both Tanner and Jodie were in trouble, and that no one, certainly not Sandy Trotter, was going to do anything about it.

His last thought before he admitted defeat was, Tanner, I'm sorry.

Chapter 18

When Tanner awoke, every muscle in her body ached. She had slumped sideways on the floor of The Booth in her sleep, and her neck felt as if someone had been stabbing it repeatedly with a sharp knife.

But what upset her most was that she had lost track of time. The two pieces of transparent tape on her toes were of no help at all. She had no way of knowing how many times the cuckoo clock had chirped the hour while she was asleep. She was very angry with herself.

Groggily, painfully, she pulled herself to her feet. She peered through the gap she'd created for some hint of what the time might be, but couldn't tell if the light she saw was daylight or artificial light.

Tanner leaned her face against the cool, rough wood. Was Sigmund even now on his way to the house? Where did he go when he left her? "Places to go, people to see." That meant that he had a life apart from the horrible torture he was putting her through. If he had friends, they couldn't possibly have a clue that he could do this kind of thing. It was hard to believe that there were people out there who smiled and waved at Sigmund, made plans with him, sat across from him at a table. If only they knew what he was capable of.

Tanner was tired. She was especially tired of being frightened, of not knowing what was going to happen next, of never knowing exactly when Sigmund might return or what he would do when he did return. But she wasn't ready to give up. "Back to work," she muttered, bending awkwardly to retrieve the metal ruler. "You had a nap, so you have no excuses. Get busy. Think of Silly. Think of Charlie. Think of Jodie, and quit feeling sorry for yourself."

She had no idea how long she worked before she heard the key turn in the lock. There didn't seem to be any point in continuing with her toe-timing, since she had no idea what time it was when she woke up. And it was impossible to tell from inside The Booth whether or not daylight was flooding the skylight. It could still have been the middle of the night for all she knew.

She had pried away from the side only a

dozen nails, leaving them in place on the back wall, when she heard the music room door open. As far as she could tell in the darkness of The Booth, Sigmund wouldn't notice what she'd been up to unless he checked closely. The back wall was still in place. Only she knew that one hefty push would separate at least the upper half of it from the left side wall. She slid the ruler into its corner on the floor beside the tape dispenser.

"What time is it?" was her first question as her arm came up to shield her eyes again from the sudden flood of light. It was morning, she realized as she stepped out into the music room. Pale sunshine filled the skylight.

"Why? You got a date?" he asked sarcastically.

She glanced up at the cuckoo clock. Eight A.M. People on campus would be getting dressed, eating breakfast, going to class if they had an eight o'clock, maybe rolling over and going back to sleep if they didn't. Oh, God, she prayed fiercely, let me go back there, let me be a part of campus again, I promise I'll never complain about my father again, never! Just let me have my life back.

Had he come to kill her? The worst part was not knowing, ever, whether or not this would be the time.

Her spine tingled.

She wanted to walk around the room to get her circulation flowing, but her feet hurt too much. She sat on the couch instead. "What have you done to Jodie?" she asked bitterly. "Is she all right?" She lifted one leg and propped it on the other one so she could examine, finally, the sole of her foot. What she saw made her ill.

"Well, if she isn't all right," he said, perching on the arm of the leather chair, "there's nothing you can do about it, right? And if she is all right, then she doesn't need you worrying, so shut up about her." He was still wearing the mask and the green plaid shirt.

Tanner's left foot was crisscrossed with jagged cuts, and caked with dried blood. The cuts were puffy and red, with angry streaks radiating outward from the wounds. Infected, she thought despairingly. I should have washed them right away. She put that foot down and lifted the right foot, the one that she had hurt again, in The Booth. It was even worse. The cuts were swollen and several of them oozed a runny, yellowish liquid.

"I need antiseptic and ointment for my feet," she said, thrusting them outward so he could see. "They're infected."

He shrugged. "That's your fault. Breaking

all that glass and then being dumb enough to step on it. By the way, you look like hell."

"Like I care," she said angrily. She sat up straighter. "You aren't feeding me, and you aren't giving me medicine. Prisoners of war get better treatment than this. It's the law. I could get blood poisoning and die, is that what you want?" Stupid question.

"Oh, stuff a sock in it. I'll get you something to eat."

"Don't forget the medicine. There's antiseptic and ointment in the medicine cabinet upstairs. I don't suppose you'd let me go up and get it, and take a nice bath while I'm up there, would you?" Her skin felt oily and grimy, and her hair hung against her shoulders like wet yarn.

"Get real," he said coldly, and left the room, locking the door after him.

Tanner closed her eyes and waited. If he brought her real food, that would give her strength. She needed strength. And if she could do something about her feet before they got any worse, she'd be able to stand longer to work on the nails.

He came back carrying a metal tray with another sandwich on it, this one peanut butter, and only a wet paper towel for her feet. No antiseptic, no ointment. "Just wash them off," he said, handing her the tray. "Don't be such a whiner. I can't stand whining."

It wasn't enough, any of it, but Tanner knew she had no choice. She ate the sandwich, hoping he'd let her get a drink from the lavatory before sticking her back in the booth.

The paper towel was not only inadequate to treat the wounds on her feet, the barest touch of it made her wince in agony. But it was all she had. She dabbed at the soles of her feet as gently as she could, and could see no improvement at all.

"You were a patient of my father's, weren't you?" she asked. "That's why you're mad. You didn't like the treatment he prescribed for you, whatever it was. So you're punishing me."

"Your father's *treatment*," he hissed, bending to thrust the gray mask into her face again, "was to send me away! Like I needed that. I came here to Salem expecting everything to be okay, better than high school, which wouldn't have been hard. High school was a nightmare. But I had a few problems adjusting here. I made the mistake of talking to some stupid counselor, and he sent me to see the ever-popular psychiatrist, Dr. Milton Leo. And that was all she wrote. After five crummy sessions, like he could know who I was after only five forty-minute sessions, he shipped me off to a hellhole known as a 'residential treatment center.' All that time, wasted! He talked my parents into approving the deal. The excuse they'd been waiting for my whole life. Ship me out, get rid of me, free them from this creepy kid of theirs. The insurance paid, so what the hell did they care?"

"My father and I aren't a mutual admiration society," Tanner said wearily, resting her head against the back of the couch, a retreat from that mask so frighteningly close to her face, "but he knows his profession. There must have been a reason why he sent you there. He probably knew what I know now, that you're violent. You . . . hurt Silly." She couldn't bear to say the word "killed." "And I know you hurt Charlie and Jodie. And look what you're doing to me." Her voice went cold and unsympathetic as she added, "No wonder my father sent you away. I don't care how horrible that place was, they should have kept you there."

That enraged him. He grabbed her hair and dragged her up off the couch. "It's because of *him!*" he screamed into her face. "I wouldn't be doing any of these things if he hadn't sent me there!"

"Yes, you *would!*" she shouted back. If she was going to die, she was going to have her say first. "You would have done it all, sooner or later. My father *saw* that, and that's why he sent you away. Only it didn't help, did it?"

"I should kill you right now, right this minute," he said, tightening his grip on her hair. Then, just as quickly, he released her. She fell backward, onto the couch. "But it's not time yet. I haven't been able to reach him, to tell him what's going on. What's the point, if he doesn't know? Of course, he can't get back here in time to stop anything, not all the way from Hawaii. But imagine what that trip will be like for him? That long, long flight, already knowing that I've got you, and that I don't intend to let you live. He'll be in his own little Booth, there on that airplane, a prisoner of his fear and anxiety. He won't be able to breathe right and he'll have chills. Then he'll start sweating like a pig and he'll think an airplane has never moved more slowly than that one. And it won't do him a bit of good. God, I wish I could be here to see the look on his face when he comes home and finds you, the way I've left you. It won't be a pretty sight."

Tanner, listening to him, hearing the hatred, and then the excitement and the triumph in his voice, felt as if she might pass out at any moment, from sheer terror. She knew that if she tried to stand up, her legs would never hold her.

"If you let me go," she said urgently, "I won't tell anyone what you did. I'll say I was staying with a friend. They'll never know you were here."

"Oh, that's brilliant," he said. "And I suppose you'll say that precious housekeeper of yours just jumped into the freezer of her own accord, right? Wanted to chill out, did she?" He seemed to find that very funny, and began laughing, watching her reaction through the tiny eye slits.

Tanner closed her eyes again. To hear him talk that way about the one person who had made life in this house bearable made her feel as if a giant vise was squeezing all the life out of her heart.

Her eyes still closed against his ugly face, she said softly, "Why don't you just drop dead?"

"I expect to get in touch with your father today," he announced. "And the minute that I do," he paused, and when he spoke again, it was with an Arnold Schwarzenegger accent, "I'll be back!" He laughed again.

When he reached out to grasp the neck of her sweatshirt to put her back in the coffin, Tanner knew she should protest. She should scream and kick and drag her feet, as she'd done before, or he might get suspicious.

But she couldn't. She just couldn't. What little energy she had left, she needed for her work inside The Booth. A plan was formulating itself in her head, and she knew now what her purpose was in pulling the nails free. The plan could work. If she got lucky. And now, ironically, getting back *inside* The Booth was her only hope. Strange, when up until now she had thought of being put inside that horrible coffin as the *end* of hope.

"Don't tell me all the fight's gone out of you," Sigmund said as he opened the door and pushed her inside. "Good. Makes it easier for me. See you later." Then, after he had closed the door and the wooden wedge had dropped into place, he chilled her blood anew by saying in a light, casual voice, "We don't have much time left, Tanner. Pretty soon, the police will have to step in and take action. I intend to get on with my life after yours is finished, so I can't afford to have the law snooping around here. Besides, I'm getting tired of putting my plans on hold just because your father decided to see paradise. 'Bye, now. Back later, I promise. Don't go away." He laughed, and a minute later, he was gone.

And she was trapped in The Booth again.

Chapter 19

Charlie didn't wake up in the infirmary until almost noon. His stomach turned over when he glanced at his watch and saw how late it was. He'd slept the entire morning away? Damn that nurse and her needle!

His first thought then was of Tanner. Where *was* she? Was she okay?

She had to be okay.

His second thought was of Jodie, wondering if Sandy had located her, and his third thought was that his body felt as if he'd been run over by a train. Everything hurt, even his teeth.

He was anxious to leave, but he was told by the nurse that he would not be allowed to go until he had been officially discharged by the doctor, who hadn't arrived yet. "And the police are waiting to talk to you," she added as she left Charlie's cubicle.

The Twin Falls police officer who came into

the room asked Charlie routine questions. Had he seen the driver of the motorcycle? No. Did he know what kind of motorcycle it was? Yes, a Harley. Did he know any reason why someone would want to run him down?

This was the question Charlie had been impatiently waiting for. He told the officer everything, from the note hanging on the mailbox to his second trip to Tanner's house, brutally interrupted by the motorcycle on the sidewalk. "I know it had something to do with Tanner," he finished. "Someone didn't want me going to her house and snooping around. You can see that, can't you?"

Noncommittally, the officer asked, "You still have that note?"

Charlie nodded. "Over there, in my jeans," he said, pointing to his clothes, folded over the back of a chair.

The officer unearthed the note, read it quickly, and turned back to Charlie. "This her handwriting?"

That was the question Charlie hated to answer. "Yes," he admitted reluctantly, then added hastily, "But she wouldn't have written that unless someone made her do it. I tried to explain that to the other officers, but . . ."

"So where exactly do you think your friend is?"

Charlie's heart leaped with hope. This officer was listening to him, which was more than the others had done. "I think she's still in that house," he said firmly. "And I don't think she's able to leave or get to a phone. If she could, she'd have called me. And then there's Jodie, Jodie Lawson," he added, "another friend of ours. She went to that house, at least I think she did, and no one knows where she is now. So could you please check it out? The house, I mean? You can get a warrant or something, right?"

The officer pocketed his notebook. "Let me get this straight," he said. "You think that two of your friends are being held prisoner in Dr. Leo's house right there on Faculty Row? With professors going in and out of their houses every day, and kids playing in the street? Don't you think that'd be a little hard to pull off?"

Charlie sagged back against the pillow.

The officer smiled. "The nurse said you might have a concussion. A blow on the head can do some mighty strange things, kid. But then," he added sympathetically, "so can being dumped by a girlfriend."

"She didn't dump me," Charlie said wearily, giving up. This guy wasn't going to be any help. Making one last attempt, he asked, "Can't you at least try to call Tanner's mother? Just check it out?"

The officer shrugged. "You said you don't remember her last name. And you don't even know where exactly she is. If you can't find her, what makes you think we can?"

"You have computers!" Charlie cried in disgust. "You're supposed to be able to find people."

"Yeah, well, even a computer needs more to go on than the fact that someone is traveling in the Orient," the man said drily. "The Orient's a big place." As he turned to leave, he said over his shoulder, "If you can remember the woman's last name, and come up with any more information on her whereabouts, let me know. Maybe I can make a phone call or two."

When he was alone again, Charlie made his own phone calls. He couldn't just sit in his bed doing nothing while he waited to be discharged. He had to do something. There was always the possibility that Tanner and Jodie had turned up while he was sleeping off the effects of that shot the nurse had sneaked into him. If it hadn't been for that, he could have been out looking all night.

Maybe his friends had done it for him.

They hadn't. Philip and Vince weren't in

their room. Sloane, when Charlie reached him, said that Philip was probably working and Vince had a class. "Sandy's frantic, though," he added, his tone of voice indicating that he couldn't understand what all the fuss was about. "She's called here half a dozen times this morning. Can't find her roomie. Personally, it wouldn't kill me if Joellen stayed lost. She's a pain in the . . ."

"Not funny, Currier," Charlie said sharply. "Jodie may not worship the ground you walk on, but she's a friend, and something's happened to her. I have another call to make, and then I'll meet you at the frat house. We'll go to Tanner's together."

"Charlie, I have classes, and my g.p.a. isn't all that great."

Charlie held the phone to his chest, rolling his eyes to the ceiling. When he spoke again, it was coldly and carefully. "Sloane, *be* there!" He hung up.

He made one more phone call. And to his relief, the next voice he heard, traveling a long distance through the telephone wires, was Dr. Leo's.

Charlie was reluctant to tell Tanner's father the truth. If he said Tanner was missing, Dr. Leo would hang up immediately and phone the Twin Falls police. And they would tell him it wasn't true. Not officially, anyway. He'd think Charlie was jerking his chain, and that would make things at the Leo house even chillier than they were now.

More important, Charlie wouldn't have learned a single helpful thing.

He made up some stupid story about wanting to get in touch with Tanner's mother to find out what Tanner wanted for her birthday.

The doctor was incredulous. "You called me in Hawaii, and you're planning on calling Gwen in the Orient to ask some ridiculous question about a birthday present? What's going on, young man? Is this a joke?"

Somehow, Charlie stumbled through the conversation long enough to discover that the ex-Mrs. Leo went by the name of Reed now, and that she was probably in some place in Japan called Kyoto. But Dr. Leo had no idea what hotel she was staying in, or if she was even staying in a hotel, adding coolly that "Gwen has friends all over the planet. She could be staying with friends in Japan, but I would have no idea what their names are. We no longer share that sort of information."

Okay, so that hadn't told Charlie much. But he wasn't ready to hang up. He had never believed that Tanner was with her mother, anyway. He had just thought it was important to know how to get in touch with the woman if necessary.

Charlie decided to take a different tack. "Dr. Leo, while I have you on the phone, this is going to sound crazy, but hang with me for a minute, okay? Do you . . . well, is there someone on campus who might have it in for you?" Enough to hurt your daughter, he added silently.

The sound that Charlie heard then sounded very much like a snort. Hard to believe, but there it was. "You can't be serious, young man. I am probably the most universally disliked teacher on that campus, as if you didn't already know that. I tell people the truth, and that is not something most people want to hear. Why are you asking me such an odd, and completely unnecessary question?"

It *was* stupid, Charlie admitted to himself. The list of people who disliked Dr. Leo could be a mile long. But, what else did he have to go on?

"Think, sir, please. Someone who made threats against you, maybe? A student with a bad grade? Something like that?"

Dr. Leo sighed impatiently. But he fell silent for a moment, and then said slowly, "Well, there was this one patient. A young man, your age, Charles. Began at Salem last year, but had so many problems, he couldn't continue. Had to be hospitalized. I've never seen a patient so angry. Filled with rage, that boy."

"But he's hospitalized, you said."

"Oh, not anymore. He was in for a year, and then his insurance ran out. Had to be discharged. As a matter of fact, he's matriculating at Salem now. He started as a freshman again, in September."

Charlie's stomach rolled uneasily. "But he's okay, right? I mean, you said he was discharged."

"Charles, some patients are discharged when they're well. Others are discharged when there is no more money to keep them in the hospital. This was the case with the patient I'm talking about. I was very much against his release, but since I wasn't willing to foot the considerable bill for his continued care, my objections were overlooked. I will say, however, that he came to me as soon as he returned to campus and told me with what seemed to be sincerity, that I'd done the right thing. His rage seemed to have dissipated, and he seemed grateful for my diagnosis and prescription. I had planned to keep an eye on him for signs of renewed mental distress, but after that visit from him, I decided it was unnecessary." Dr. Leo paused, then added, "I wasn't wrong, was I?"

"Can you tell me that patient's name, Dr. Leo?"

"I suppose that wouldn't be breaking confidentiality. I'm sure there are other students on campus who are aware that he was hospitalized. Those things aren't exactly kept a secret on a college campus."

Then he told Charlie the name of the angry patient.

Into the silence that followed, Dr. Leo added, "I'm convinced this young man bears me no ill will, Charles. Why are you asking? Has there been some vandalism to my property?"

Charlie didn't answer. He was still too stunned.

"Charles?" The doctor's voice changed, took on a note of genuine concern. "Is my daughter all right? Has something happened to Tanner?"

Charlie returned to awareness. Tanner would have been surprised to hear the worry in her father's voice. She wasn't certain how he felt about her.

"No," Charlie lied. Why make the man frantic when he was too far away to be of any help? Any *more* help. He'd already done more than he knew. "She'll probably call you later." Charlie prayed he was right. He hoped that Tanner would be *able* to call her father later. "Thanks for your help," he said sincerely.

And then headed as quickly as possible to the frat house.

Charlie had been wrong about the police officer. He had indeed taken Charlie seriously, but had seen no point in alarming Charlie further. Two girls not where they were supposed to be? That wasn't something to be taken lightly. The officer knew about the seventy-two hour rule, but didn't hold much stock in it. If a person was missing, the trail could get pretty darn cold in seventy-two hours.

A drive past the Leo house, maybe a walk around the perimeter couldn't hurt. The doc, who the officer knew wasn't the most popular guy in town, had once helped with a problem with the wife, who was having a hard time with nightmares. Knowing the limitations of a small-town police officer's salary, the doc had charged very little for his services, which had been successful. Officer McKeon felt he owed the man. No, a little side trip to Faculty Row couldn't hurt.

He found nothing unusual on the outside of the house or on the grounds. The surveillance cameras seemed to be working, and there was no sign of a break-in.

But since he was there, might as well go inside. Had a skeleton key, could use that if he had to. Was surprised to find the back door unlocked.

The doc wouldn't have gone off to Hawaii and left a back door unlocked.

Curious now, the officer went inside. The house was quiet as a tomb. Not a sound anywhere. The girl couldn't be here, like her friend thought. Cameras in every room, she'd have seen a police officer arriving. If she was being held here against her will, she'd be screaming and shouting her lungs out now, to get his attention.

But there wasn't a sound.

Hand on the gun at his side, he checked every room, opening doors, closing them when he found no sign of life in them. Listening intently the whole time for a sound, a voice. Heard nothing.

The only room he didn't check was one at the front of the house, on the left side of the hall. Tried the door, rattled the knob, but it wouldn't budge.

Must be that music room Officer McKeon had heard about. Valuable instruments and manuscripts in there. Soundproof, too, he'd heard.

Doc kept it locked up tighter than a safe with the queen's jewels in it.

Shaking his head at such measures, the officer took one last look around, and left by the back door.

If he noticed a scrap of yellow and rust fabric hanging over the edge of the closed freezer lid, he thought nothing of it.

Officer McKeon left the Leo property satisfied that the young man in the infirmary had been misguided. There was nothing unusual going on inside that house.

He was almost to his car when a tall, stocky young man in a green plaid shirt and jeans ambled by, giving the officer a friendly smile and a casual wave.

Officer McKeon waved back and got into his car.

The campus was full of young men exactly like the one passing by.

Like I said, he thought as he pulled away from the curb, nothing unusual there.

Chapter 20

Tanner was never aware of Officer McKeon's presence in the house. She heard nothing, and since she was inside The Booth, she didn't see him on the surveillance screen.

Unaware, Tanner continued to work diligently on painstakingly prying the nails loose from the side walls, leaving them intact in the back section of The Booth. She hadn't stopped since Sigmund first pushed her inside early that morning. She hadn't bothered to keep track of the time. It didn't seem important. She was going to continue doing what she was doing, as fast as she could do it, so what difference did it make whether she had only a little time or a whole lot of it?

The metal ruler was beginning to make groaning sounds when she slid it into the gaps and pried the nails upward, and she was terrified that the tool was about to snap in half. She'd been working it very hard. Without it, she had no hope at all.

Tanner was very tired. Her head ached. She had been standing for hours, her weight pressing the swollen, infected soles of her feet into the rough wood. The pain never eased. Her skin itched. She felt sticky and sweaty, and had to constantly brush her oily hair away from her face. Finally, in exasperation, she snapped off a long piece of Scotch tape from the dispenser, yanked her bangs away from her face, and slapped the tape against them to keep them out of her eyes. "It won't make the fashion magazines," she muttered aloud as she turned her attention to another nail, "but it works. That's all that counts."

The thought that kept driving her in spite of her exhaustion and pain was a strong, certain belief that Sigmund didn't intend to let her live through the night. He had said the police would be called in soon, and he didn't want them "snooping around." Although Tanner had no idea why the police hadn't already arrived when her friends knew she was missing, she had concluded that it probably had something to do with the note Sigmund had pinned on the mailbox. If the police saw that note, they'd assume she'd left the house of her own free will. So they wouldn't be willing to look for her, would they?

Eventually, though, and Sigmund had to know this, the truth would come out. Someone, probably Charlie, would learn that she wasn't with her mother, after all, and then the police would have to act. That was what Sigmund was worried about.

Convinced that she had very little time left, Tanner's sore and swollen fingers moved as swiftly as she could manage.

She had alternated between sides, prying away half the nails on the upper left side of the rear wall, then half on the upper right side, so that she could push away the upper half just enough to get some air. It seemed to Tanner that after being confined to this tiny, dark, airless place, she would never again have enough air in her lungs.

The upper half of the rear wall budged only a little when she pushed against it, the wood unyielding, unbending. But the gap she had created along the top half of both sides gave her more light, made it easier for her to work on the bottom half of the rear wall.

I'm crazy, she thought as she used the metal ruler as a lever. I'm as crazy as he is. This is never going to work, never. I could have this back piece almost all the way off, even be on the very last nail, and he could walk in and catch me. All of this hard work will have been for nothing, I'll be dead, and he'll probably bury me in this stupid box!

But she had to keep going. Some stubborn core deep inside of her wouldn't let her stop. "So what if he catches me?" she asked the metal ruler as she slid it beneath yet another nail-head. "At least I didn't give up without a fight."

She went on working.

It seemed like days, months, years, before she pulled the very last nail out of the side wall, leaving it intact in the rear wall. But she still had to separate the back section from its ceiling and floor.

That was easier. Sigmund had done those last, and had been very sloppy. It didn't take her that long.

When the last nail had been pried upward, Tanner's hands were sore and swollen and the tips of her index fingers and thumbs were bleeding. She didn't care. She had done what she set out to do.

She was proud of herself for not crying, for not dissolving into a puddle of saltwater on the floor of The Booth. In spite of the pain she was in, it felt good to be taking charge of her life, no matter how futile her efforts might be. She felt a tiny bit less like a victim.

Her heart told her it wasn't going to do any good. Sigmund was so much stronger than she was, especially now, when she was so weak and tired. He'd be here soon, and she didn't have a chance against him. Not really.

But, she'd tried.

Charlie would be proud of her.

She felt feverish. Blood poisoning, because of her feet? Probably.

Maybe it was just the stuffiness of The Booth.

Carefully, gently, Tanner pushed against the now-detached rear wall of The Booth, still perfectly aligned next to the sides, just as it had been before she pried the nails free of the side wall. If he walked in this very minute, she thought, Sigmund wouldn't be able to tell that I'd done anything. It doesn't show.

But in the next second, as she pushed harder, the wall came free of the sides and slowly tipped backward, then just as slowly fell to the floor.

Holding her breath in awe, Tanner watched it fall. Air rushed in to meet her, and she almost smiled.

But there was no time to waste. This was

only the first part of her crazy plan, if she could even call it a plan. A hope, that's what it was, a crazy, bizarre hope born out of desperation.

Only a half-finished hope at that.

She was so very tired. All she really wanted to do was lie down on the soft, thick carpet and close her eyes. She needed to rest. She needed hours and hours, maybe days of rest.

But not now. There wasn't time.

Taking a deep breath, Tanner stepped free of her coffin.

Chapter 21

When Charlie hurried into the frat house, Tom Wylie, sitting in the living room, called out to him. "Message for you, Cochran."

Impatient with the delay, but hoping against hope that it might be from Tanner, Charlie ran over and grabbed the small piece of paper. It told him that a Sergeant Cleary from the Twin Falls police department had called and wanted to see him as soon as possible. "*Important*" was scrawled across the bottom of the note in Tom's hen-scratch.

"Can't I just call him?" Charlie said, anxious to get to Tanner's house.

Tom shook his head. "Nope. Made that very clear. Something he wants you to see, he said. Better get your tail down there, Charlie." He grinned. "What'd you do, rob a bank? That how you got that sling on your arm?"

Tom knew nothing about Tanner being missing, or how Charlie had broken his arm. This was no time to fill him in. Thanking him for taking the message, Charlie ran up the stairs to Sloane's room. He didn't know what to think. Maybe this Sergeant Cleary had good news for him about Tanner. Or maybe he had discovered, as Charlie had, the identity of someone who just might know where Tanner was.

But . . . Charlie's steps slowed . . . the police believed that Tanner had left town of her own free will on some fun-filled jaunt to the Orient and therefore hadn't been searching for her. So how could they know anything? Anything *good*? Wouldn't any news they had be *bad* news? Something that had accidentally come to their attention, like a . . . a body?

Oh, God, what was he thinking? He was *not* going to think like that. Besides, the police didn't just call when they found a body, did they? Didn't they at least come in person to deliver that kind of news? On television, they did.

Sloane was in his room, but there was no one with him. "Couldn't raise Philip and Vince," he said. "Sorry." He looked sullen. "I missed a math test, by the way, waiting for you. Have to make it up on Monday."

"Where's Sandy?" Charlie barked, unsympathetic to Sloane. Sloane just wasn't used to not having his own way, that was all. He'd get over it. "Why isn't she here?"

"How should I know? I can't keep track of everyone. I called Sandy's room, and there wasn't any answer. Maybe she's out looking for Joellen. So, are we going to Tanner's house or not? I've got another class in half an hour."

"Forget it," Charlie said brusquely. "We have more important things to do. C'mon, we have to go into town."

Sloane looked unhappy. "All the way into town? What for?"

"Police station. Sergeant there wants to see me. I think he has news about Tanner. Come on, Sloane, quit dragging your heels. I'll drive. Then, unless something that sergeant tells us changes my mind, we're going straight to Tanner's house."

"Well, I hope that sergeant knows where she is and that she's fine and dandy, Charlie," Sloane said grimly, although he left his chair and grabbed a jacket out of the closet. "Because you're driving everybody nuts thinking something's happened to her, when all that probably happened is that Tanner decided to escape from that father of hers. I don't blame her," he groused as they left the room. "Who'd want to live with him?"

The car seemed to Charlie to crawl toward

town, even though he pressed as hard on the accelerator as he dared. The town police were always on the lookout for college students speeding. The distance between campus and the village had never seemed longer.

It took him an extra five minutes to find a parking space near the police station.

By the time they ran inside the police station, Charlie's head was pounding. This was taking up so much valuable time, when he could be in that house looking for Tanner. Or on campus checking out a discharged mental patient whose name he now knew. Whatever the sergeant had to tell him had better be worth the trip.

There were four people ahead of him, tending to business of one sort or another with the desk sergeant. The man at the head of the line was arguing loudly, and it didn't look like he was going to give up any time soon.

But when an impatient Charlie went to another officer to ask for help, he was waved back to the desk at the front of the room. Clearly, no one received help without first going through the desk sergeant.

Charlie paced back and forth, watching the minutes pass on a large round clock at the front of the room.

When he thought he couldn't stand it any

longer, and that nothing Sergeant Cleary could tell him would be worth wasting all this time, the last person left the line and he was finally facing the desk sergeant.

"Sergeant Cleary, please," Charlie said. "I'm Charlie Cochran. Sergeant Cleary asked to see me."

The desk sergeant lifted his head from papers he'd been working on and looked at Charlie. "Today? Cleary wanted to see you today?"

Charlie nodded. "Yes. He left a message saying it was important. Something he wanted to show me."

The sergeant shook his head. "I don't think so. Cleary didn't call you today. He's in Norfolk, Virginia, at a seminar. Left Monday. Won't be back until Saturday afternoon. Doesn't seem like he'd be calling you from Virginia. You sure you got the name right?"

"I didn't take the message," Charlie said impatiently. "Someone else did. But that's the name he wrote down. Cleary. Sergeant Cleary."

"Well, he's not here. Hasn't been. Won't be. Someone gave you a bum steer, kid. And what is it that you think Sergeant Cleary would be wanting to see you about? Maybe I could help."

But Charlie was already running from the police station, dragging Sloane along with him.

Charlie was shaking his head and muttering, "I don't believe this, I am such a fool! What a total idiot!"

He did not obey the speed limit signs on his way back to campus and Faculty Row.

Chapter 22

Out of the coffin, Tanner wanted nothing so much as to relish her freedom. She wanted to run around the room, leaping for joy, touching things, breathing in the air, staring up at the brilliant blue sky above the skylight.

But she didn't dare. No time. She'd been lucky so far. He could turn the key in that lock at any second, and there would be the back wall of The Booth lying on the floor. She would never survive his anger.

Bending painfully, Tanner lifted the back wall and aligned it once again along the side walls. When it was in place, she picked up the heavy Scotch tape dispenser and wielded it as a hammer, knocking the nails back into their holes in the side walls. It wasn't important to get them in perfectly, or even all the way, just enough to hold the back wall in place. That would be enough if her plan worked.

While she was hammering frantically, she tried to keep her eyes on the screens high up on the walls for some sight of Sigmund. That was difficult, because she had to keep her eyes on the nail holes as well.

She finally gave up on the screens, telling herself that it was more important to finish her task.

She had two more nails left when she heard the key turning in the lock.

Grabbing up the metal ruler from the carpet, she threw herself into the empty woodbox beside the fireplace and drew the lid down on top of her. She had just shut out the last tiny bit of light when the door opened and Sigmund called out, "Pizza, anyone?"

In her hiding place Tanner shook so violently, she was sure he'd see the woodbox trembling and come to see why. She could smell the pizza. It smelled heavenly, tormenting her hungry stomach and reminding her of fun afternoons and evenings at Vinnie's, with her friends. She made a face of disgust. He was going to feed her now, finally, when he was about to kill her? Sick! He was so sick! No wonder her father had had him put away. She'd like to get her hands on the person who had let him out.

She was listening so hard in an effort to keep

track of his movements, her ears ached with the strain.

She heard the sound of the pizza box sliding onto the coffee table in front of the couch. Then soft, whispery footsteps on the carpet, moving . . . moving where? Tanner tilted her head, pressed her ear up close against the front of the woodbox. Footsteps moving toward The Booth? She had to pay attention, had to know exactly when he was standing directly in front of The Booth with the door open. He wouldn't be able to see the woodbox then. The door opened to his right and, once fully open, would hide the woodbox from his view.

"Come out, come out, wherever you are!" he sang cheerfully, and she knew he was at the door to The Booth. That wasn't enough. He had to *open* it, so he couldn't see her climbing out of the woodbox, couldn't see her coming from behind the open door, sneaking up behind him . . .

She heard the wooden latch twist, and, blessedly, the coffin door creaked as it swung open.

"What the hell . . . ?" she heard him shout and knew he was staring, probably open-mouthed, into the empty booth.

She tumbled out of the woodbox, jamming the tape dispenser between the top and the lid to prevent any slamming sound when the lid fell. Then she jumped up and ran to The Booth, rounding the open door and coming up behind him.

He was still standing there, staring into The Booth, and never heard her coming.

She threw out her arms, hitting him between the shoulders with all the force she could muster. He didn't fall. She knew he wouldn't. He was so much heavier than she was. But he was completely taken by surprise, and uttering a startled oath, he lurched forward, off balance.

Quickly, she shoved again, and because he hadn't yet regained his balance, this time he stumbled all the way into The Booth.

Tanner slammed the door shut and twisted the latch into place.

Then she stared at The Booth, disbelieving.

It had worked.

He was trapped.

Chapter 23

When Sigmund was safely inside the coffin that he himself had built, Tanner let out a triumphant cry.

But she wasn't safe yet. That back wall wasn't on all that securely, she knew that. Right now, he was pounding on the door, which she'd expected. But when that didn't work, he just might turn his attention to the back wall, and see the gaps she'd seen. It wouldn't take him any time at all to knock that back wall free.

She wouldn't be safe until there was no way for him to escape. None.

He was stronger than she was, and The Booth itself weighed something. But if she couldn't do this last part, it would all have been for nothing, because Sigmund would, sooner or later, free himself.

She stood back, a short distance from The

Booth, and taking a deep breath, threw herself at it.

The Booth shook, but that was all.

That wasn't what she wanted. It wasn't enough.

Five times, Tanner stepped away from The Booth, each time going farther and farther away, and although she was hampered somewhat by the sorry condition of her feet, tried to run straight toward the box, throwing her complete weight against the door, her goal to tip it over on its back.

The last two times she tried, it did tip slightly, but always steadied itself.

She probably never would have succeeded if it hadn't been for Sigmund himself. It didn't take him long to figure out how she had escaped. Sigmund, Tanner knew, wasn't stupid. Crazy, but not stupid. When she heard him banging against the back wall, she knew he'd realized how she'd made her escape, and was attempting to do the same thing himself. It would be much easier for him than it had been for her. He was stronger, and the wall was no longer attached very securely.

Tanner was sick with disappointment. And fear. Not only was he going to get out, after all her hard, painful work, but he'd be so furious when he made his escape, she probably only had a few more minutes to live.

It was then that she noticed The Booth shaking, and realized what he was doing. He had noticed that the wall wasn't as firmly attached now, and he was throwing his full weight against it in an attempt to remove the wall completely.

She knew it wouldn't take him more than two or three tries to break free.

But . . . if she could time it perfectly, if she could guess when he was about to fling himself at that back wall, and do the same thing herself against The Booth from the outside, their combined weight might do exactly what she wanted.

If she hadn't been so terrified that it wouldn't work, she would have laughed aloud. Because if it *did* work, Sigmund himself was going to help her trap him. That seemed so wonderfully ironic, so perfect . . .

Still, if it didn't work, she wouldn't be laughing. She wouldn't be doing anything. She wouldn't be anything . . . except dead.

The Booth shook again, and it seemed to Tanner that the back wall of The Booth made a faint ripping sound. Some of the nails pulling free? One or two more tries, and Sigmund would be at her throat.

She backed up, away from The Booth, counting in her head, and then, when she thought the time was right, made an awkward stumbling, almost-running jump, ignoring the pain in her feet, and threw her body, full force, against The Booth — at precisely the same moment that Sigmund threw his body, full force, against the back wall.

The Booth tipped, tilted, and then fell slowly, heavily, onto its back, making a soft whooshing sound as it landed on the thick carpet.

Tanner stood, paralyzed, at one end of The Booth, staring down at it. Now it really did look like a coffin again, lying on its back like that. Sigmund was screaming from inside it, screams of outrage and disbelief.

She couldn't believe it, either. Her crazy, insane plan had worked. It shouldn't have, but it had.

He couldn't get out now. The back wall was pressed into the floor, his weight and the weight of The Booth on top of it, making it impossible for him to remove the wall as she had done.

Tanner finally snapped out of her awe. Time to leave, to get out, to run to freedom, while he was trapped inside that box.

She stumbled gleefully toward the door. She

would have run, but her feet were bleeding and she had to walk on her heels.

He was still screaming with outrage when she got to the door.

And realized, with a lurch of her heart, that she wasn't going anywhere, after all.

Because she didn't have the key to the music room door.

He had it.

In his pocket.

Inside the coffin.

Chapter 24

Tanner didn't know what to do. She couldn't get out of the music room without that key. There was no telephone, no way to call for help before Sigmund found a way to escape his prison. Her only hope was to get out of the room. But how was she going to get that key?

The door to The Booth was on the top now, where she could easily open it. But if she did, and reached in to try pulling the key from his pocket, he'd grab her and choke the life out of her.

Tanner leaned against the music room door. So close to freedom, she was so close, and now . . .

There was a new sound now, combined with Sigmund's furious shouting. The sound of something heavy hitting wood. His feet . . . kicking at the floor of The Booth . . . he was going to kick his way out?

Tanner remembered how easily she had removed the ceiling, because Sigmund had done the ceiling and floor last and hadn't been that careful. That floor wouldn't hold for long against his strong, angry kicks.

Hesitantly, Tanner moved closer to The Booth, wincing each time Sigmund's work-booted feet slammed into the floor. She could already see a crack in the boards. She stood watching with dread as the box shook with his rage and his determination to be free of his coffin, the one he had constructed for her, not for himself.

He would be free in minutes.

And then . . .

A board in the floor of The Booth shattered, then, a moment later, another splintered and cracked and shattered. Two of the smaller boards were still intact. He'd make short work of those, and then he'd be wriggling his way free, feet first.

Feet first . . .

Tanner kept her eyes on The Booth. She had one chance now. Only one . . .

He was coming out feet first.

The key was in his jeans pocket. That was where he always put it.

His feet, his legs, his jeans, would emerge

first, before the powerful arms that could choke or pummel the life from her.

His *jeans* would come out first.

The jeans with the pocket.

The pocket with the key.

They would emerge from the box first.

And she'd be there, waiting. She would only have a second or two, no more than that.

Scarcely breathing, Tanner moved closer to the floor of the coffin and crouched, conscious of pain in both feet. She waited, her heart in her throat.

Two more solid kicks, and the floor was gone, her end of The Booth surrounded by shattered wood.

Here came his feet now, the workboots pushing their way through the hole he had created.

Every nerve in Tanner's body was on alert.

Now his ankles, his shins, his legs . . .

She held her breath and leaned closer, closer, her right hand extended, waiting, waiting . . .

Mumbling triumphantly, he pushed again, scooting forward quickly, so quickly . . .

His thighs, his hips . . .

There! the side pocket she had seen him slip the key into each time he came back into the music room. And there it was, the metal tip of it sticking half out of the pocket, right there, so close, so close . . .

Tanner's right hand shot out, yanking on the key.

It stuck.

They both screamed at the same time, he with rage, feeling the movement at his pocket, she with frustration.

The key was stuck on something inside his pocket.

He was still wriggling, faster now, it seemed to her, shouting and cursing the whole time. There was his belt buckle, emerging.

Shaking, fighting tears of frustration, Tanner pulled with superhuman strength on the thick metal key.

She heard a ripping sound.

Sigmund shouted at her.

But the key came free.

So did Sigmund's lower chest and his fists. But his arms were still pinioned inside the coffin.

Clenching the key in her own fist, Tanner leaped up and raced for the door. She thrust the key into the lock.

Upside-down.

Ripped it out, spun it right side up, thrust it in again.

Scuffling sounds behind her. A satisfied gasp that told her he was free.

She turned the key.

"Oh, no, you don't!" he shouted, and she whipped her head around, saw him on the floor, free of the box, saw him jump to his feet, aim for her . . .

"Oh, yes, I do," she said. The doorknob turned in her hand. She grabbed the key free, yanked the door open, and jumped into the hall. She was about to pull the door closed when she saw him, halfway across the room, yank off his mask.

Tanner froze.

She knew that face. Strong, good-looking, with nice eyes when they weren't behind a nasty mask. Kind eyes, she had thought when he showed her around campus in late August. Kind eyes, she had thought when he told her which were the best places to eat and where to do her laundry and what hours the library kept. She had thought he knew all those things because he'd taken a summer course at Salem. Now she knew that wasn't why. It was because he had started school here a year ago. Then his education had been interrupted by emotional problems, problems for which her father had prescribed care in a residential treatment center.

This year, supposedly treated and cured, he'd returned to continue his education. To start over, begin his life again, make new friends. Friends like her, and Charlie, and Sandy, Vince and Jodie and Sloane.

The face Tanner saw, twisted with anger and hatred, belonged to her good friend, Philip Zanuck.

The shock of seeing the face of a friend froze Tanner's movements. It wasn't until that face, almost unrecognizable in its fury, was only a foot away from hers that she remembered what she had to do.

He screamed, "You don't know what it was like! Being trapped, being caged!" and lunged for the door.

"Yes, I do!" she shouted back, and slammed the door shut. Before he could shove it open again, she stuck the key into the lock and turned it.

She sagged against the door. Philip? Philip. So that was why he'd hated her father.

She might have dated Philip, if she hadn't met Charlie.

She moved away from the door, toward the foyer, so exhausted the slightest movement was an effort.

She was free now.

She was safe.

The pounding that she heard then wasn't Sigmund, wasn't coming from behind her, from the music room door. It was coming from the front door. Someone was pounding on the front door of Dr. Leo's house.

She knew, even before she opened it, that it was Charlie. He had come, at last, to save her.

But she'd already done that herself.

Tanner, her back and shoulders very straight, her head high, walked slowly, painfully, to the front door to open it.

Epilogue

Tanner lay in a long, narrow, white bed in the infirmary with her feet, cocooned in thick layers of white, sticking out from underneath the blanket. Her face was no longer flushed with fever, and she smiled as she looked up at Charlie, who sat beside her bed holding her hand.

Jodie, found tied and gagged but alive in the basement of Dr. Leo's house, lay in the bed next to her. Other than several ugly bruises on Jodie's chin from a rough landing when Philip had tossed her into the basement, she was in good shape.

"I still can't believe Philip would do such awful things," Sandy said for the fifth or sixth time.

Tanner groaned. They had discussed Philip so thoroughly, she had reached the point where she never wanted to hear his name again. "Well, he did," she said curtly. "And every time he left me, he went straight to the frat house and did everything he usually did, so that no one would suspect him. Even borrowing the motorcycle from the garage where he worked didn't raise any suspicion, because he'd done it before. His boss didn't mind."

"I keep thinking about how surprised I was when your dad gave me Philip's name," Charlie said soberly. "I couldn't believe it. Thought he'd made a mistake. But when he said how angry Philip was about being sent away, how he'd threatened your father with revenge, I knew that whatever was happening to you was because of Philip. I shouldn't have wasted time going to the police station like that, but I was hoping they'd found out where Philip was hiding you."

"I saw him on the motorcycle that day," Sloane volunteered. "That day you were hit, Charlie. But I never once connected Philip with your . . . accident. I knew he sometimes borrowed bikes from the garage, but I never had a clue that he'd deliberately run someone down. I mean, Philip never even got into fights. He never seemed mad at anyone. I sort of envied how cool he was."

Tanner nodded. "We all thought that. It was exactly what he wanted us to think. Philip is very, very clever."

"Ah, but so are you," Charlie said with admiration.

"This is true," Tanner said, smiling. She knew the nightmare of being trapped in that horrible box would stay with her forever. Forever. But that didn't mean she had to let it ruin her life.

"He seemed so normal," Sandy mused aloud. "I always thought psychos had wild hair and eyes and talked to themselves all the time. Philip wasn't like that. Everyone liked him."

"He's sick," Charlie reminded her. "And you can't always tell that when you look at someone, not even someone as sick as Philip."

"Can we *please* stop talking about him?" Tanner cried, moving restlessly in her bed. "I don't want to think about it anymore, okay?"

Charlie nodded. "You're right. Philip is where he's supposed to be, put away in a hospital for good, and you're safe. That's all I care about."

"So, when does your father arrive?" Jodie asked Tanner.

Sloane, standing at the foot of the bed with Vince, made a face of distaste. Ignoring him, Tanner replied, "This afternoon. I still can't believe he took the first plane out after he talked to Charlie."

"He was really worried," Charlie said. "I

could tell. I knew the minute he gave me Philip's name that you were in serious trouble, but I didn't say anything to him. He just guessed, that's all."

Sloane snorted. "You're not going to make a hero out of him now, are you, Tanner? Just because he's interrupting some dumb conference to rush to your side?"

"*And* his vacation," Tanner pointed out. "No, Sloane, I'm not going to canonize him. But I just might stay in that house, after all." She turned her head toward Charlie. "It's weird. When I was trapped in that room, I thought all I wanted to do was get away from there, and never come back. But now, I figure the worst has already happened, right, and I got through it. So what's there to be afraid of now? Of course," she added softly, sadly, "Silly won't be there. That's the worst part."

"She'd be really proud of you, though," Charlie said, squeezing her hand. "Like everyone else. Even your father."

"Then maybe," Tanner said, a slow smile returning, "maybe I'll try to talk him into turning that music room into a family room. Think he'll go for it?"

"Oh, wow," Sloane said eagerly, "party time!"

Tanner laughed.

About the Author

"Writing tales of horror makes it hard to convince people that I'm a nice, gentle person," says **Diane Hoh**.

"So what's a nice woman like me doing scaring people?

"Discovering the fearful side of life: what makes the heart pound, the adrenaline flow, the breath catch in the throat. And hoping always that the reader is having a frightfully good time, too."

Diane Hoh grew up in Warren, Pennsylvania. Since then, she has lived in New York, Colorado, and North Carolina, before settling in Austin, Texas. "Reading and writing take up most of my life," says Hoh, "along with family, music, and gardening." Her other horror novels include *Funhouse*, *The Accident*, *The Invitation*, *The Fever*, and *The Train*.

Return to Nightmare Hall . . .
if you dare

Deadly Visions

I can't believe she saw it. The last person I would have expected.

There they were, all of them, gathered around the painting, not one of them suspecting there was anything unusual about it.

And then here she comes, this little nothing who knows squat about art, and announces the truth.

I could have strangled her, right then and there, with my bare hands. Probably should have. Wish I had.

No, that's not true. Right there in public, in the middle of a crowd? Losing my cool would have ruined everything.

Well, if I don't stop her, she's going to do exactly that, Ruin everything.

No problem. Of course I'll stop her. That insignificant little ignoramus isn't going to spoil all my fun.

I'll see her dead first. The little twit won't live to see another Monday.

How shall I do it?

Something clever, something truly . . . artistic.

THRILLERS